MURDER
IN THE MERLOT

AARON STANDER

WRITERS & EDITORS
INTERLOCHEN, MICHIGAN

ISBN: 978-0-578-13685-1

Printed and bound in the United States of America

FOR BEACHWALKER

WHO HELPS THIS ALL HAPPEN

1

~

Sheriff Ray Elkins guided his patrol car—strobes on the overhead light bar flashing—along the twisting ribbon of the state highway that snaked around the shoreline of Cedar County, a long thin peninsula that extends into northern Lake Michigan. He glanced across the quiet water in the bay, then slowed and turned inland. He left the level shoreline and climbed into the rolling interior—countryside covered with orchards, vineyards, and farms. He worked his way through a maze of narrow asphalt roads, slowing as he turned onto Pelkin Hill Road, a washboard of gravel and potholes bordered on each side by fencerows thick with underbrush.

At the base of the hill he brought the vehicle to a crawl, then carefully turned onto a two-track and threaded his way through two fieldstone columns, an old wooden gate angling away from one of them. He stopped near the rear of an old rusting Chevy pickup. As he climbed from his car, the door of the pickup swung open.

"Ray," said Marty Donaldson, as he moved toward the back of his truck.

"Are you okay?" asked Ray, starting to take in the scene. Donaldson was breathing in short, quick gasps. His face was flushed, the front of his blue cotton work shirt darkened with perspiration.

"Such a shock…"

"Are you okay?" Ray asked again, noting the stainless steel bracelet with a caduceus hanging from Donaldson's left wrist.

"I just need to catch my breath."

"Dispatch said you found a body."

"It's just beyond that car."

Ray leaned away from the truck and peered at a red Audi sedan. "Man, woman?"

"See for yourself," answered Donaldson, cementing himself against the back of his pickup.

Ray looked at the area beyond the vehicles and braced himself. This was the one area of police work he struggled with, confronting death.

He walked past Donaldson's truck and the Audi, wet with the thick morning dew. He found the body a few yards beyond in the grass and weeds at the side of the dirt lane. A female form was face down. Most of the torso was covered by a bright red dress in a shade similar to the color of the sedan. He crouched near her head, noting the long blond hair and silk scarf as he reached around the woman's neck with his index and middle finger to palpate for a pulse. The skin was cool and moist. Ray knew she had been dead for hours. He stood and carefully surveyed the body. As he backed away, he noticed a crimson stiletto shoe laying off to the side of her left foot.

Returning to Donaldson's side, Ray said, "Tell me exactly what happened."

"After breakfast I ran down here to check on the merlot grapes. I've been doing this morning and night for close to a week. They're almost ready to pick. The first thing I find is that the gate is open." He motioned with his right hand in the direction of the gravel road. "We don't lock it or anything. But we keep it closed when we're not working in here, mostly to discourage kids from parking here at night, you know, beer cans and cigarette butts. Not that it happens a lot, but once a summer is enough if you're the one who has to clean things up.

"The next thing I see is that car," he pointed over his shoulder in the direction of the Audi. "Then I check the car. It was covered with dew, couldn't see much through the windows. So I'm thinking it's been here for a while, maybe all night. I open the door. It's empty except for a few things on the passenger seat. Then I start looking around. The first thing I noticed was the dress. The bright red.

I moved closer to get a better look. I reached down and touched her skin. She was cold, way cold. I think I sort of freaked out. I yelled at her, hoping she'd wake up. I think I was sort of in shock, not making much sense."

Donaldson paused, working to catch his breath. "This is the stuff of movies. I couldn't believe it. It took me a few minutes to comprehend what was really happening. Then I went back to the truck and called 911." Donaldson pulled himself into a seated position on the bed of the truck, resting one arm over the right side. A pair of washed out jeans extended to the top of his worn work boots. His head was covered by a faded green baseball cap with a soiled block "S" at its center.

"My evidence tech and the medical examiner are on their way, Marty. While we're waiting, I've got a few routine questions we can work through."

"I'll do my best," Donaldson leaned against the inside of the truck box.

"Did you see anyone or any cars on your way here this morning?"

"No. Early morning. Nothing much is moving yet. Don't think I saw anyone between our place and here."

"This woman, have you ever seen her before?" asked Ray.

"I don't think so. It's not like I took a good look at her, and I couldn't see her face much, but no. Did you see those shoes? Not up north."

"Any possibility she might have visited your tasting room or winery?"

"Possible, but if she did, I wouldn't have seen her. I don't get in there much during harvest time. My wife and daughter-in-law mostly look after those things this time of year."

"How about the car? Have you seen it around?"

"No."

Ray looked up at the carefully terraced hillside where long rows of grapevines clung to evenly spaced trellises that ran across the steep slope. "How long have you had this property?" he asked.

"I bought it about ten years ago. Couldn't afford it today. Since our big, multinational neighbor arrived, land good for grapes has skyrocketed." He paused, "It was just an old orchard with mostly dead trees when I started. I had to clear them out, bulldoze the terraces, build the trellises, and do the planting. So much work, Ray, over lots of years. But it looked like the perfect terroir for reds, so I planted it with merlot and cabernet franc. My hunch was right. We're starting to make great wine from this hillside."

He looked directly at Ray. "And now this. I don't understand. Why here? Why in my little corner of the world?"

2

When the first road patrol unit arrived, Ray escorted Marty Donaldson to the passenger side and held the door open for him. "Share with your wife what's happened and try to relax. I'll need to talk with you again."

"When can I get started harvesting?"

"Possibly later today, Marty. Tomorrow for sure."

Ray bent down and looked past Marty to the young officer behind the wheel. "Run Mr. Donaldson back to his house. And, Brett, I want you to walk him in." He closed the door and watched the deputy reverse out of the two-track and head up the gravel road.

He was running the plates on the Audi when Detective Sue Lawrence, his young second-in-command, arrived. Elkins gave her a quick summary of his conversation with Donaldson as they stood at the back of her Jeep. After pulling a camera from its padded case, she asked, "Did you check the body?"

"Briefly. I felt for a pulse. The body was cold. She's been there for hours. I had a quick look around and got out of there. I didn't want to mess up your scene."

"You actually touched the body?" she asked.

He gave her an affirmative nod.

"Any signs of violence? Wounds, blood…"

"I don't think so. I didn't linger," he answered as he led her past the Audi and pointed to the patch of bright red in the tall grass.

Ray stood back and watched Sue photograph the area around the body, admiring her efficiency. The sun was just breaking the top of the ridgeline, warming the hillside, burning the dew off the grape leaves—most cloaked in late-season dull green, some already turning to yellow. He could smell autumn in the air, leaves at the early stages of decay.

The click of the shutter was occasionally muffled by the sound of traffic from the distant county road, a north-south artery that ran along the center of the peninsula. Sue carefully moved around the body, staying back a half-dozen or more feet and getting photos from various angles.

Finally coming to Ray's side, she said, "I'll get more photos when Dyskin starts his examination."

"See anything?"

"Nothing remarkable about the body. And there's not much else to work with here. No footprints. No litter of any type." She looked at the Audi. "Do you have a name?"

"Gillian Mouton. New York City address. Googled her. Only one Gillian Mouton in the U.S. Apparently, she's some sort of wine expert."

"Let's look over the car while we wait for Dyskin."

They walked around the Audi, wiping away the dew to look into the windows. Keys dangled in the ignition. A purse lay on the passenger's seat. An iPhone rested next to the purse on the gray leather upholstery.

Their attention shifted to the rattles and groans of an approaching vehicle on the rough gravel road. The medical examiner's ancient Lincoln Town Car slowly turned into the vineyard. Dr. Dyskin, a nylon running suit hanging on his narrow frame, emerged from the car. He retrieved some coveralls from the interior, then perched on the driver's seat and slowly pulled them on, first one leg, and then the other. Ray looked over at Sue. He could see her impatience with Dyskin's leisurely pace.

Finally, Dyskin rummaged around in the cavernous back seat and retrieved a black baseball cap. "What do we got?" he asked as he approached them.

"A woman, probably in her early thirties. No obvious injuries," answered Sue. "The body is just ahead," she said, leading the way.

Ray watched the process many yards back. Dyskin carefully examined the body, starting with the scalp and methodically working his way to the feet. Ray could hear Dyskin muttering to himself as he went. Then he rolled the body over and repeated the process, paying special attention to the area around the neck. Sue captured every aspect of the exam with her camera.

Eventually Dyskin slowly stood. He bent over and brushed the soil from the knees of his coveralls. Picking up his bag he came to Ray's side, Sue following closely.

"I'd say ten to twelve hours, based on body temperature. I probably can get it a bit more accurate by looking at the overnight temperatures. I'd say sometime between ten and midnight, give or take an hour either way. The body got a name?"

"We're working on that. The Audi was rented to a Gillian Mouton."

"Nice name."

"Cause of death?" Ray asked.

"Only speculation at this point, only speculation. I could find no wounds, fractures, nothing of that sort. And this doesn't look like an OD or anything of that nature. I'm curious about the neck area, not too obvious, but...."

"The silk scarf. Could that have been used as a ligature?" asked Sue.

"I don't think so. I mean, if you used a piece of silk like that, pulling it really tight, wouldn't it...? What I'm trying to say is it looks like it's just been ironed. It doesn't appear to have been strained or distorted in any way. This looks like a strangulation, I'm wondering about a chokehold."

"Chokehold?" asked Sue.

"Used to see a lot of those in the bad old days. Used to be common practice by law enforcement to subdue uncooperative suspects. Problem was, suddenly they'd have a body on their hands, but there was no visible trauma to the area. They'd usually try to pass it off as a heart attack. We'd identify the real cause of death during the post."

Dyskin looked at Ray. "Very suspicious death, Elkins. Send this one to Grand Rapids for a forensic autopsy. Pity. Very pretty woman, even in death."

"Any chance the body was moved?" asked Ray.

"No. Look at the position of the limbs. My guess, she was strangled and dropped. She met someone here. They walked a few yards, and she was grabbed from behind. Let's see if the autopsy proves me right about the chokehold part. I've bagged her hands, lovely set of claws, nary a chip on the paint job. Don't think they'll find anything. The perp cut off the blood to her brain. It was over real fast. If my theory is correct, you're looking for a cold-blooded killer. Shooting someone is relatively easy, killing up close…the perps are really damaged. Be careful."

Dyskin looked back at the body for a long moment. "If you can't find anyone local to ID the body, her kind will have dental records."

Ray walked Dyskin back to his car. As Dyskin was pulling off his coveralls he said, "You don't like bodies, do you?"

"I've never gotten used to it, starting with my first night in a patrol car when I had to help pull a badly mangled teenager out of a tree after he crashed his motorcycle."

"The early ones are the hardest." He paused for a minute and put his arm on Ray's shoulder. "The population of the planet turns over every hundred years. That's the reality. Our job is to get justice for people like this woman who didn't get their fair share of years. And that part you and your impatient young friend are very good at."

3

~

"I've ordered a tow truck. I'd like to get this car to a secure place so I can process it later," said Sue Lawrence as she scanned the exterior of the Audi. "That said, let's get the phone and her purse."

Sue retrieved a cardboard evidence bin with assorted paper bags from her Jeep and penciled in the site, time, and location on one large and one small bag. With Ray's assistance, she placed the phone in the smaller of the paper bags and carefully finessed the purse into a larger one, placing each bag into the bin. Then she gently lifted a soft, black sweater from the seat, exposing a manila folder. After opening the folder and inspecting the contents, Sue looked over at Ray. "Almost too good."

"How so?"

"It's all here, everything, starting with her flight numbers and rental car confirmation. Then there's the information on her local lodging."

"Where was she staying?" asked Ray.

"The Manitou Resort, Eagles Nest condos. Probably has a great view of Lake Michigan."

"What else?"

"It's her day-by-day schedule, everything. The list of wineries she was visiting, addresses, and contact names. She also has time slots with labels like *blog, Facebook,* and *e-mail.* This woman was a highly organized workaholic. Sixteen-hour days, nothing was left to chance."

"Almost nothing," observed Ray. "How about yesterday afternoon?"

She looked back at one of sheets in the folder. "Ursidae Winery in the afternoon. Early dinner with Phillip Lovell."

"Anything else?"

"She has a work period scheduled from 9 P.M. to 11 P.M. Then the schedule resumes this morning at seven, again a time designated for *Desk Work* with winery visits starting at 11 o'clock."

"Are Marty Donaldson or the Terroir Nord Winery on the list?"

"Yes, Terroir Nord is mixed in with lots of others scheduled for Monday and Tuesday."

"We'll have to pursue that later. We need to talk with Phillip Lovell," said Ray. "But before we do, I'd like to get a search warrant and check her condo. We need to secure anything that might be helpful. Obviously, she's got a computer there. I don't want it to go missing. How about the trunk?"

Sue toyed with the remote until the lid popped. A small backpack and a pair of hiking shoes rested at the center of the carpeted space.

Sue inspected the shoes carefully, one at a time. "High quality, seem to be broken in."

Then she looked at the contents of the backpack. "Jeans, shirt, hoodie, small camera, flashlight, and a container of Mace."

"So she was probably here to meet someone," said Ray. "She was going to change her clothes. But what was going to follow? What were her plans?"

"She should have carried the Mace on her person," said Sue, returning it to the backpack.

The two-story condo rented in Gillian Mouton's name consisted of one large room on the first level with a kitchenette tucked away in one corner and a carpeted stairway that led to a loft bedroom. The lakeside wall of the unit was glass, floor to ceiling.

"What an incredible view," observed Ray, moving toward the windows. "You can see the entire length and breadth of the Manitou Passage."

"Two wine glasses on the table, one with lipstick," said Sue, focusing on the task at hand. "And the remains of a roach on a saucer, again with lipstick. And her computer." She opened the cover on the MacBook Air. "Well, that's handy, she didn't bother with a password." Sue perused the page. "She was working in Word." Her eyes scanned the text. "Looks like the draft of an article or blog entry on Michigan wine."

Closing the cover again, she scanned the area. "We've got the empty glasses. Where is the bottle?" She moved around the kitchen area. "Not on the sink or counter…or in the trash."

"I'll check the fridge," said Ray. He opened the door and looked into the interior, then peeked into the freezer. "Lots of wine, none of it has been opened. There's nothing else. No food and no stash of drugs in the freezer." He looked across the counter that divided the kitchenette from the rest of the main room. "So we know she entertained someone here. I wonder what time?"

"I would bet before dinner, if she went to dinner."

"Let's do a walkthrough."

"I'll get these prints and bag the roach. You look around."

A few minutes later Ray leaned over the loft railing. "There's something up here you should see."

"Ah, the missing wine bottle," she said after ascending the steps. "Champagne bottle," she corrected as she moved closer. "So we have the empty bottle on the floor, rumpled sheets. I wonder if this is one of her wine pairings?"

Ray dropped to his knees and read the label out loud, "'Sparkling wine from estate produced Vignoles grapes in Cedar County'. Excellent choice. I served you some of this last Thanksgiving."

"I remember," said Sue. "Same wine, different results."

Ray let her comment hang as he thought back to that evening when they both had had too much champagne. Now he was glad he had held back. His young colleague was so important to him both professionally and personally. A love relationship would probably not have worked out well for either of them in the long term.

Ray pointed to an iPad mini on the nightstand.

Sue folded back the cover. "No password on this, either. Looks like she was shooting video." She moved her gloved finger across the touch screen. "Have you ever met Phillip Lovell?"

"I think I've been introduced a time or two. Community events. A bit corpulent and rather loud as I remember."

"Do you recognize him in this video?"

Ray tried to hold back a smile. "Like I was saying, he needs to spend more time in the gym."

"And I didn't know you could blush," Sue said.

"Can you determine the time?" said Ray.

"Yesterday, late afternoon." She moved to a menu, "There are seven bits of video," she said, launching the second clip.

"It looks like they were taking turns playing videographer."

"Yes," agreed Sue. "Two distinct points of view, both male and distaff."

"We assume the iPad is Gillian's?"

"Just a couple of more clips, then I'll check." A moment later Sue was looking at the e-mail menu. "Gillian's iPad. These are all her e-mail accounts."

"Are there other videos? Was this some sort of high-tech belt notching?"

Sue looked at the photo library. "There aren't any more video clips. In fact, very little else, just pictures of wine bottles, vineyards, that sort of thing. If Gillian was given to collecting...what should I call them...moments to remember...perhaps she was moving them to a thumb drive for archival purposes." She gave Ray a mischievous smile, "Or perhaps this video was only intended for instant replays."

"You can finish up here later," said Ray. "We need to get over to Ursidae Winery and have a chat with Phillip Lovell."

"Let's hope he hasn't decided to leave the country."

Ray looked over at Sue, "Now you're blushing."

"I've never interviewed a person of interest where I've had such an intimate knowledge…"

"Take the iPad along," said Ray, "in case Lovell needs to have his memory refreshed on where he spent yesterday afternoon. But keep it under cover until he starts to hang himself."

4
~

Sue parked near the front of the large, recently constructed tasting room of the Ursidae Winery.

"Do you like this place any better, now that the landscaping is done?" she asked.

"It's muted the effect a bit. That said, the building remains a confused conglomeration of periods and styles."

"Have you had any of their wine?" asked Sue as they walked toward the entrance.

"No," said Ray. "I've heard their reds aren't too bad. But I've been put off," he gestured toward the building, "by the Disneyesque exterior. Can you make great wine in bad architecture? It's a karma thing."

After they flashed their IDs and asked to see Phillip Lovell, a uniformed hostess made a quick phone call and then guided them through the crowded tasting room. The interior was clad in dark wood. Artifacts of wine making, mostly European in origin, decorated the walls above the two long bars that ran along opposing walls. Carefully positioned spotlights illuminated the sampling and sales areas.

Servers, male and female, in white shirts and buttoned black vests, provided small pours of the featured vines to clusters of patrons who lined the bars. A well-rehearsed patter accompanied each pour. The back wall of the room was decorated with the front quarters of large wooden barrels, each bearing the name of a famous French chateau deeply branded across the front.

At the back of the room, their guide pulled open a carefully obscured door and held it for them. As they stepped from the dusky interior of the tasting room to the brightly lit factory floor, their guide observed, "We call this the three century jump."

Ray slowed for a minute, allowing his eyes to adjust to the light. He scanned the interior of the large room with its array of stainless steel tanks, pipes, pumps, computer screens, and the tall, spotless white walls. Lovell's office was just beyond the entrance.

Lovell came out of his seat as they approached the open office door, coming around his desk and extending his hand. "Sheriff, good to see you again. And Ms.?"

"This is Sergeant Lawrence, she heads our investigations division."

After they were seated, Lovell asked, "What brings you to Ursidae? Not official business, I trust."

Ray looked across the desk at Lovell and wondered what was going on behind the cheerful exterior.

"Mr. Lovell, are you acquainted with Gillian Mouton?"

"Sheriff, everyone in the industry is acquainted with Gillian, the infamous Wine Bitch," Lovell said in an understated British accent. "You saw the billboard out front? She's doing an event for us in a few days. I'd be happy to comp you some tickets. She's a breath of fresh air, a real break from the stodgy lot who've dominated this business for decades. She makes wine fun and glamorous at the same time." Lovell brushed back his long blond hair, exposing more of the weathered skin on his face.

"I guess that was a long answer to a rather simple question. I have a tendency to do that. So what about Gillian? Is she in some kind of trouble?"

"I'm sorry to have to tell you this, Mr. Lovell, but Ms. Mouton was found dead a few hours ago." Ray focused on Lovell as he delivered the news, watching the other man's reaction.

Lovell sat silent for several moments. "What happened? An accident?"

"At this point it's an unexplained death. We'll know more after the autopsy."

"We found Ms. Mouton's calendar among her possessions," said Sue, opening the manila folder. "It looks like she spent yesterday afternoon here."

"Give me a moment, please. I'm just stunned by the news." Lovell rocked back and looked at the ceiling, then slowly met Sue's gaze. He wiped away a tear and reached for some tissue. "Yes, that's right. She spent the afternoon here. First, I gave her the grand tour, everything. We started with the vineyards, and then we did a top to bottom tour of the winery, from the crusher to our bottling line." He reached for another tissue.

"I'm sorry," Ray said, thinking about crocodiles' ability to shed tears at will. "So after the tour, what then?"

"We were back here. She was right where you are sitting, Ms....?"

"Sergeant Lawrence."

"Yes, exactly, right where you are sitting. A stickler for detail, she was. Took everything into account. No margin for error. She does, did, the best events in the industry. Drew a different crowd, a new generation of wine drinkers."

"So after your meeting, according to her schedule," Sue had her finger against a point on the page, "you went to dinner?"

"We went to dinner later. I think it was about 5:00. I had a few things around here that needed attending to. She went back to her condo to change. Our plan was to meet in Traverse City at 6:30."

"Why didn't you share a ride?" asked Ray.

"We both had other plans for later in the evening. We were going to have dinner, then go our separate ways."

"And is that what happened?" asked Sue. "We're trying to establish a timeline for her movements yesterday."

"Yes, we had dinner at the Cooks' House. Gillian was a champion of regional cuisine and local wines. I think the restaurant is an exemplar of that concept."

"So you didn't accompany her to the condo?"

"Like I was saying, we arranged to meet in town."

Sue pulled the white iPad mini from her pack and set it on the desk. She looked directly at Lovell and asked, "Was the champagne from this winery?"

Lovell cleared his throat, and then toyed with a ballpoint for a few seconds. Lifting his gaze he said, "Uh…no, one of my competitors, we're not there yet."

"And the grass?"

"Not mine. I don't smoke…you know what I mean."

"Not even a puff?" pursued Sue.

Lovell pushed back in his chair, "Maybe a puff. We were having a glass of bubbly. Kicking back a bit."

"And then?"

"Obviously you know. And after… it was just like I told you. She followed me to town. We had dinner."

"At the Cooks' House?"

"Exactly, we had dinner and went our separate ways. She said she had some things to do."

"She wasn't more specific than that?"

"Not at all."

"About what time was that?"

Lovell chewed on a knuckle, "I can't say exactly, sometime after 8:00, maybe closer to 9:00, when we said our final goodbyes."

"And you didn't see her after that time?"

"No."

"How well did you know Ms. Mouton before this meeting?" asked Ray.

"Casually, for three or four years. Our paths would cross at trade shows two or three times a year."

"You were never in a relationship with Gillian?" asked Sue.

"Nothing like that. We've had a casual affair over the last… maybe two years. No tomorrows, no strings attached. I think she was using me for my knowledge and connections in the industry."

"And what were you…?"

"The company of an extraordinary woman. It's a real ego boost to have a beautiful young woman on your arm." He paused for a minute, and then looked directly at Ray. "There's no crime here, Sheriff. Sex between consenting adults, even in the American provinces, is not illegal as far as I know."

"Did she come to visit you here in Michigan?"

"I wouldn't say she came to visit me. With Gillian it was always about business."

"So she was here before?" said Ray.

"Just once. She came out for a few days this past June. She wanted to see the facilities she would be using for her event. Gillian was always about planning. She seemed to have some familiarity with the area. I think her family may have come here on holiday when she was a child."

"This trip, when did she arrive?"

"She came on Sunday. The event was scheduled for this weekend. She was planning to stay on a few days after."

"For what purpose?"

"I don't know. She didn't say. Probably just getting material for her website."

"And after?"

"She said something about Europe. I'm not sure where exactly. I won't say she was secretive, but she only told you what you needed to know. Nothing more."

"We need to go back to last night," said Sue. "After you two parted, did you see anyone who could provide you with an alibi for later in the evening?"

A long silence followed. "If you must know, I was visiting a woman friend."

"Does this woman friend have a name?" asked Sue.

"It's complicated, she's married. Her husband was out of town."

"We need a name and phone number, Mr. Lovell," said Sue.

Lovell sighed, picked one of his business cards from a crystal bowl on his desk, scribbled something on the back, and passed it to Sue. A second later he reached for the card, trying to pull it from her hand. Sue pushed his arm away with her other hand.

"The card, I'd like that back, please," said Lovell.

"Sorry, we need to talk to her. It's to your advantage that we do."

"I don't know much about American law, but I think I should have an attorney before I say anything else. How about the video?" He started to reach across the desk.

Sue quickly pulled the iPad beyond his grasp, returning it to her backpack.

Lovell stood. "Please know this, I was not involved in any way in Gillian Mouton's death, and I can't imagine why anyone would want to kill her. If there is nothing else, please excuse me. I've got a lot of work to do."

After they came to their feet, Sue said, "Sir, there is one more thing. Would you be willing to identify the body?" She glanced at her watch. "Let's say we meet at the entrance to the emergency department at 4:00. This will only take 5 minutes."

Lovell was slow in responding. He glowered at Sue. "Right. 4:00 o'clock," he finally said.

"What do you think?" asked Sue, once they had settled back in her Jeep.

"I'm not sure. He did seem startled by the news. If he was just blowing hot air, he's a fairly accomplished actor. What's your take?"

"About the same," She started the engine, then looked over at Ray. "As to the lying about sex—everyone lies about sex. The same is true with drugs. I bet he showed up with the joint. She wouldn't have carried any with her. Not on a plane."

"Think he'll show to ID the body?" asked Ray.

"Absolutely. It's the safest course."

5

After a late dinner, Ray walked the trail through the nearby forest in the rapidly fading light. He turned toward home as the last of the day gave way to night. Although he was carrying a small flashlight, he worked at navigating in near darkness. The trail, mostly sand, followed a twisting path through the rolling terrain. Occasionally breaks in the overhead canopy helped him traverse the path in the semidarkness.

Normally, his attention would be on the sounds, shapes, and scents of the woods at night. This evening images of Gillian Mouton drifted across his consciousness.

Back at home, he dropped into a chair and Googled Gillian Mouton on his iPad. He clicked on the top item, opening her website. A few seconds later he was confronted by the glowing face of a stunningly beautiful woman. Her eyes were fixed on the camera, her head slightly rotated, showing off her delicate features. Ray gazed at the screen for several minutes, wondering about this woman. Her expression was warm, open, and alluring.

Ray thought about King Duncan's line from Act One in Macbeth:

There's no art to find the mind's construction in the face...

He wondered about the person beyond the attractive exterior staring back from the screen. What had motivated her killer?

He toggled on a video, and Gillian came to life. "Welcome to my website, and welcome to the exciting world of wine...."

Ray watched and listened. Gillian's delivery was poised and polished, her mellifluous tone warm and engaging. He sensed how quickly Gillian could establish an intimacy that transcended the small, glowing screen.

Over the next hour he followed Gillian on tours from the storied wine producing areas in France, Germany, Italy, and Spain to vineyards across the globe, some with ancient lineages, others less than a decade or two old. Ray noted the professional quality of the videos, the superb camera work, and the carefully crafted final production.

Gillian was at the heart of every scene, asking informed questions about grapes, vintages, and production methods. Often the answers from the experts were supported by video that enhanced their explanations.

Ray also noticed that while her dress from scene to scene and video-to-video changed, there was a consistency in style. When Gillian was in the vineyards and wineries, she was clad in tight jeans, hiking boots or green wellies—depending on the weather. Her fitted shirts were preppy and always unbuttoned enough to show ample cleavage. If the temperature demanded raingear, fleece, or down, Gillian was a cover girl for Patagonia. Her evening wear also reflected a consistency of style—soft fabrics, exquisite tailoring, and a subtle sensuality that Ray thought amped up the whole effect. Stilettos, usually in a color that matched the dress, completed each ensemble.

Ray clicked on the button that opened Gillian's blog and scrolled through the entries in a random manner, stopping when his interest was piqued by a topic or photograph. He was struck by her keen sense of humor and her strong literacy skills. The blog was chatty in tone and engaging. Ray could see that Gillian was focusing on an audience of young, hip, professional women. He almost felt like he was eavesdropping on a conversation.

He searched the blogs for anything that might have engendered anger or hostility. He found no cattiness, or sarcasm. Generally, Gillian was providing counsel to her readers on how they could discover wine they enjoyed. She couched everything in terms that suggested that her readers should be their own final arbiters of taste and quality. Her mission was only to empower them.

The blogs were as much about lifestyle as wine. Ray was drawn to comments on food and pairings with different wines. Gillian's tone was playful, skillfully using the occasional sexual allusions, double entendres, and other forms of language play.

He scrolled back to the top, looking at the most recent entry he had skipped over.

Fall in the Loire Valley is especially lovely. Great wine, sumptuous food, and luxurious accommodations provide the perfect backdrop for a sizzling romantic romp. But if you're in the American Midwest—Chicago, Cincinnati, Cleveland, Detroit, St. Louis, and all those burgs in between—don't despair, much of the splendor of those fabled foreign climes is close at hand; a few hours by car or plane will take you to the splendors of Michigan's Gold Coast, the northwest shore of Lake Michigan.

Resorters have proclaimed this region's beauty for more than a century. Sadly, on the food front, progress has been glacial. Until recently the region's only contribution to the culinary world was cherry pie, which I've found in most iterations to be somehow both an overly-sweet and overly-tart pastry with fruit floating on a gelatinous, starch-based effluence, all of the above supported on a more-raw-than-cooked crust—an industrial-grade combination of flour and hydrogenated oils, no trace of sweet cream butter. The region's other culinary achievement seems to be fudge—don't even get me started.

But all is not lost. In recent years a foodie fifth column has slowly been infiltrating the realm. Fine restaurants, wine bars, and boutique breweries are popping up across the region. Artisanal food producers—bakeries, cheese makers, confectioners (not fudge)—and coffee roasters are to be found in almost every small town.

But the wine, you ask, is there any worth drinking?

A decade ago, there wasn't much. Today that industry has been transformed by a huge infusion of cash and expertise. Climate change has allowed for the planting of a greater range of varietals. And now that these vines are maturing and producing larger yields, a stunning array of new wines are coming to market.

When I scouted out the region's wineries earlier this year, I was impressed by the skilled integration of cutting edge technology with best traditional practices of the world's most hallowed producers—stainless steel tanks in one room, new oak barrels in the next, everything impeccably clean. Additionally, the local winemakers are an experienced and highly trained lot. And they continue to be influenced by the celebrity winemakers who jet in from time to time to work their magic with some of the more chichi wineries.

I think I can safely say that you won't get a bad bottle of wine from the region's better producers. But is there any great wine? Stay tuned. The Wine Bitch is on the prowl.

Ray scanned over the blog a second time. He loved Gillian's humor. He put the pointer over an item at the far right of the screen and clicked. A new window opened.

HAVE WINE, WILL TRAVEL

Hire me for:

- Corporate events

- Wine and Food Literacy classes, anywhere in the world, schedule early

- Trade show representation

- Food festivals

- The Ultimate Weekend Retreat

- Gourmet travel (Fluent in French, English, Japanese, Mandarin, and Spanish)

- The Ultimate Bachelorette Bacchanal—wine, food, and pampering in exclusive settings

- Stock your cellar, expert consulting or turnkey

Sorry, guys, this is NOT an escort service.

He switched off the iPad and sat for many minutes. First he remembered touching the cold, lifeless body. Then he reflected on the thoughts and pictures of the vibrant woman who flashed before him on the small screen.

"Why is this woman dead?" he asked an empty room.

6

~

Early the next morning Ray was in his office starting to pull together the early threads of the murder investigation. Sometime after the beginning of normal business hours, his secretary, Jan, arrived with a fresh flask of coffee.

"Remember the lockdown drill at the high school is in less than an hour," she said.

"How could I forget? You've gotten really good at handling my calendar and scheduling reminders. Maybe you'd like to do this drill for me?"

"Sorry, Ray, that's not the way it works. I know you're jammed. Why don't you have Sue do this one for you?"

"She is chasing down possible next of kin before we go public with the name of the victim. We'd like to have that done before the press briefing this afternoon."

"And then there's the budget review meeting with the county board at 10:30. You're going to be pushing it."

"Shouldn't be a problem. Plus, they always creep through their agenda. Everyone's got to have a say. But if you could invent a reason for me to be unavailable…."

Shortly before 9:00 Ray parked near the main entrance of Cedar Bay High School. The school complex—three separate buildings: elementary, middle, and high—stretched along a quiet side street at the back of the village. Athletic fields covered a large expanse at the rear, ending in a wooded area that was bordered by a country road.

Pulling open one of the six doors at the main entrance of the high school, he entered the building and was greeted by Maggie Engle, the district's veteran superintendent and high school principal. They retreated to her office to quickly review the Michigan State Police Guidelines for a shelter in place drill.

"Which scenario are you using?" asked Ray, looking at the guidelines.

"Let's start the year with the hardest one," said Engle. "Active shooter in building. And I want to start the drill about two minutes after the hour when the kids will all be in halls heading to their next class. We've practiced all the possibilities. Now it's time to see if anyone was listening."

She passed Ray a clipboard holding the official documentation form, then handed him a pen. "Just in case you forgot to bring a writing instrument. Where do you want to be, at least in the beginning?"

"Central hall, near the front door and staircase."

Engle glanced at her watch. "We better get moving. I've programmed the drill to start two minutes into the break."

As the class change bell sounded, doors exploded outwards and the corridors were quickly filled with the loud chatter of hundreds of teens. Ray watched the high-energy parade passing before him. Most of the boys were clad in t-shirts and jeans. The girls seemed divided between jeans and skirts, some in t-shirts, others in blouses. A small minority, both male and female, were in shorts, and some of those in flip flops.

"Not the dress code you remember," observed Engle.

Ray chuckled. "Is there one?"

"Absolutely. Feet and intimate body parts must be covered at all times. No obscenities or racial slurs on clothing or skin."

A warning tone sounded over the PA system. The cacophony of voices rose momentarily in response to it and then fell again.

"Lockdown. Shelter in place," a stern male voice said. "Lockdown. This is a drill. Lockdown. Shelter in place. Lockdown. This is a drill." The announcement came a second time, and the halls started to empty, students scurrying into classrooms, their voices fading, teachers, custodians, and other adults helping direct the process. The halls quickly emptied, and the building became eerily quiet.

"How are we doing?" Engle asked.

Ray looked at his stopwatch. "Forty-eight seconds. Gutsy of you to do a drill during a class break."

"Might as well go for the worst case scenario," said Engle. "Most of these incidents seem to happen when the kids are on the move. We could probably do this in less than twenty seconds if all we had to do was lock the doors and huddle the students in corners away from windows. There would be a few stragglers, but most of them would be quickly tucked away."

Ray looked again at his watch, "A minute and change. Your staff, the kids, everyone knew what to do. Let's do a quick walk-through before you end the drill."

They traversed the long corridor, checking to see if each classroom door was locked and peering in to see that everyone was out of the sight line of the windows. Then they scanned an empty lunchroom and moved on to the gymnasium. A few basketballs were scattered on the shiny oak floor of the otherwise empty and silent space. Ray checked the doors leading to the locker room. "Everything is secure."

At the far end of the building they pushed through the double doors into the auto shop. "Where are the kids here supposed to secure?"

"The tool crib," Engle answered as she walked to the back of the room. Ray watched her try the handles on both doors.

"Amazing," she said. "Not a sound. These are boys you can't keep quiet. And there's not even a hint of cigarette smoke. Absolutely miraculous." Because her school district was small and she had come up through the ranks as a teacher and principal, Engle knew her schools and the students well.

They went outside and surveyed the area at the back of the building before they climbed to the second floor and checked the remaining classroom doors.

"Perfect," said Ray as they descended the stairs at the front of the building. "Give the All Clear, and I'll sign off on the paperwork."

A few minutes later, seated in Engle's office, Ray said, "My compliments. That went like clockwork."

"Yes," said Engle. "And you know what's interesting, fire drills—tornado drills, too—it's so hard to get the kids to be serious. But a lockdown/shelter in place, even though they know it's a drill, they are completely serious. There's no clowning around. The kids shut up and follow directions. You saw it. I think many of them, perhaps most, have internalized this nightmare scenario, the active shooter in the building. They've seen it too many times on TV, kids running from a school with their hands on their heads, SWAT teams standing at the ready."

"It's one of my nightmare scenarios, too," said Ray, cupping his coffee mug. He focused closely on Engle seated across from him. She looked smaller, grayer, and more fragile than he remembered.

"I know you've done a lot of training with your staff and students. We've done the same within our department and with other law enforcement agencies in the region. We've learned a lot since Columbine and subsequent incidents. Still, standing in that hallway, watching everyone do the right thing…."

"I know what you're going to say, Ray. With only one shooter, we could have a catastrophe in five or ten seconds. All our training and procedures might do little more than minimize the carnage."

"Yes, that's the fear. And to a large degree, it's beyond our control."

"Fortunately," said Engle, "this is a small school. We've worked to stay close to all our students, with special attention to the troubled ones. That said, you just never know, it could be any kid, an academic or athletic star. Adolescents struggle with so many things." She took a sip of coffee. "And then all the guns. Almost every home in the county has shotguns, deer rifles, pistols. How many are adequately secured?"

"Not enough," said Ray.

Engle sipped her coffee and then held Ray in her gaze. "I've worked to stay connected with each new generation of students. The world is rapidly changing, but adolescent behavior is fairly constant. A lot of their parents walked these halls not so many years ago. I look at their kids and see them as just the next iteration. But now that I'm the age of most of their grandparents, I feel like they look on me differently, like I'm some kind of relic of a former age. I'm starting to think about retiring."

"What would you do?"

"I don't know. That's the problem. This has been my life, especially since my husband died. How would I adjust to the quiet? What would an angst-free environment feel like?"

"Don't make any hasty decisions," said Ray. "I can't imagine the district without you."

"I've just let the 'R' word loose in my psyche. It's sort of exciting, actually."

7

Sue Lawrence slowed and carefully checked the number on the mailbox. She wasn't comfortable depending on her GPS. She stopped at the base of the long gravel drive and peered up at the white frame farmhouse that stood near the top of the ridgeline. Her eyes scanned the plastic laminated sheet on the top of her clipboard: *Protocols for Death Notification.* She looked over the list a second time, and then slid the sheet under the other papers attached to the board.

As she slowly crept up the drive, Sue rehearsed how she would establish whether or not Gregory Mouton was related to Gillian Mouton. If it turned out that they were related, she visualized how she would tell him of Gillian's death. While she had performed this unpleasant duty a number of times during her relatively short career, it never became routine or less painful.

Sue looked for a doorbell. Finding none, she knocked on the screen door, an elaborate piece of Victorian woodworking that, like the rest of the porch, was in need of repair and paint. In the soft light beyond the screens, she could see pieces of old wicker furniture. A door beyond the porch opened to the interior.

She knocked a second time, louder and longer than the first. A large cat dropped off one of the couches, looked her way briefly, and disappeared into the house. Seconds later, Sue was confronted by a petite woman in a cotton blouse and jeans. She could see that the woman was startled to see someone in uniform at the door.

"Yes, Officer, is there some problem?"

"I'm looking for Gregory Mouton. Is he available?"

The answer was slow in coming. "Yes. I'll call him. What's this about?"

"May I come in?"

"Yes, certainly. What does this concern?"

"I'll explain when he's here. You're his wife?"

"Yes, Sherry Mouton."

"I would like to talk to the two of you. Is there a place we can sit?"

"Why don't you come into the kitchen?" She turned toward the interior. "Gregory, there's someone to see you."

A large man came down a stairway that opened into the kitchen. To Sue he appeared to be much older than his wife. Once they all settled around the kitchen table, Sue directed her comments to Gregory. "I found your name in Gillian Mouton's address book. Are you related?"

"She's my sister, my stepsister. We're estranged. We're not really in contact. What's the problem?"

"I have some bad news. Gillian Mouton was found dead yesterday."

"Where?"

"Here in Cedar County."

"How did she die? Accident I imagine. She was always totally reckless."

"Her body was found in a vineyard. At this point it is an unexplained death. We are just beginning our investigation."

Sue looked toward Gregory, then toward his wife. They appeared shocked by the news, but in the quiet that followed, she didn't detect any grief—no tears, sobs, or other expressions of loss. She did note that the Moutons locked eyes for a number of seconds and wondered what intelligence might have passed between them.

Sherry Mouton broke the extended silence. "We don't know anything about her. She made it clear years ago that she didn't want to have anything to do with us. That was okay on our part." Sherry looked over at her husband and continued, "We don't know anything about her, do we Greg?"

"No," he responded, as if on cue, "we haven't heard from her in years."

Sue pulled Gillian's driver's license from an envelope and slid it across the table to Gregory. "Will you confirm Gillian's identity based on the photo and other information on this document?"

Picking it up, he examined it carefully. "That's her alright. I heard she had been living in New York for awhile." He pushed it across the table to his wife. She looked at it briefly and handed it back to Sue without commenting.

"Do you know of other relatives that should be informed of Gillian's death?"

"I don't know," Gregory answered. "Her mother was my father's second wife. My father was pressured to adopt Gillian early in the marriage. He continued to look after Gillian's welfare and education after the marriage was over. As to her mother, I heard she died. I think it was a few years after she divorced my dad."

"Possible spouses, children, other relatives?"

"I know she was married once," said Gregory. "Never met the man. My father heard that the guy was someone she picked up at Vail. She was starting an MBA. The guy moved to Ann Arbor, bought a big house. They split about the time she got her diploma. Never heard about kids. That's all I know."

Sue thought about other questions she wanted to ask, but held back. They could wait for another time. Passing business cards across the table, she said, "If there's anything we can do, please call. That's my direct number."

"Miss," said Sherry Mouton. "We can't be held responsible for funeral expenses or anything like that just because we're sort of family?"

"No. Not at all." Sue stood, feeling that she should say more. After a long silence, she said, "I'm sorry for your loss." As she made her way back to her Jeep, she reflected on how empty that phrase sounded, especially when they didn't seem to care.

8

~

After leaving the school, instead of heading straight for the highway, Ray slowly cruised one of the old neighborhoods in the village. The streets and lawns were dappled with sunlight streaming through the variegated foliage of the mature trees. Most of the modest, well-kept homes that lined the streets dated back to the earliest days of the village, when the virgin forests still fueled the region's economic engine.

Leaving the village, Ray headed west a few miles and turned onto the access road that led to the Cedar County Government Center: a modern two-story complex faced in red brick that consolidated all of the county's agencies in one location. The site, almost invisible from the highway, had been carved out of a second-growth forest.

It was almost 10:30 when Ray dropped into a chair in the board meeting room. He arrived just in time to see Commissioner Melvin Feilen cast the one negative vote on the final budget for the road commission.

Ray remembered Feilen from high school. Feilen was a senior when he was a freshman. Feilen—tall and wiry back then and always in black, including a heavy leather jacket most of the year—was rumored to be the meanest kid at Consolidated High. Feilen disappeared into the Marines at graduation, and Ray didn't encounter him again until he, too, returned to Cedar County.

"Let's move on to the Sheriff's Department, now that the Sheriff is with us. I understand you have been at a lockdown drill at the high school," said Charlotte Frederickson, Cedar County Board Chairperson. "I want you to know how much we appreciate your

41

proactive leadership with the department. Will you join us please," she asked, motioning toward a table in the front across from the commissioners.

"Ladies and gentlemen," she began, "I want to remind you again that we are dealing with a final budget. You have had numerous opportunities to question Sheriff Elkins on specific items during budget subcommittee meetings. And I'm sure you are aware of the fact that the department's budget numbers have changed very little over the last several years. Are there any final questions or concerns before we move this item to a vote?"

"I have one," said Melvin Feilen, not waiting to be recognized. "There was a piece on last night's news about a body being discovered here in the county. Would you fill us in on this? Apparently you haven't gotten around to holding a press conference yet."

"Commissioner Feilen, I'm sure we share your interest. That said, could we...."

"This should take a few minutes. And it speaks to the broader question of transparency. If there is a killer loose in the county, the public deserves to know."

Frederickson exhaled loudly as she looked over at Ray.

"Sir," said Ray, looking directly at Feilen. "A body was discovered yesterday, and we reported that at a press briefing yesterday afternoon at 4:30. Currently, we are attempting to contact the next of kin and are in the early stages of the investigation. We have another press conference scheduled this afternoon. At that time we hope to be able to provide the name of the deceased."

"We are talking about murder here, aren't we, Sheriff?"

"We are awaiting autopsy findings."

Frederickson rapped her gavel. "You had your question, Melvin. Can we get back to the matter at hand?"

"Absolutely," he responded without waiting for the chair's recognition. "First, let me remind all of you that the original constitution for the State of Michigan stipulated that local county sheriffs had but one function, and one function only—to provide a jail. Since that time, one big government addict after another has piled on more and more money wasting functions. Most of them have little or nothing to do with running a jail." Feilen stood and lifted a bundle of papers over his head and shook them. Ray noticed that the tall thin kid he remembered was now sporting a bit of a gut. Feilen's hair was still black, but seemed unnaturally so. Ray scanned the other commissioners. They appeared bored by Feilen's theatrics.

"Just look at this," Feilen said, both the volume and pitch of his voice rising dramatically. "The jail is little more than a footnote in the department's budget. There's the road patrol, the marine unit, a school liaison officer, community policing, animal control, etc., etc., etc. What this budget tells me is that big government is alive and well in Cedar County. Most of these things," Feilen lifted the budget document again and waved it in the air, "his department does our citizens could figure out for themselves if government just got out of their way. My constituents would prefer to keep their hard-earned dollars rather than have big government invading their lives. They'd take a 20% cut in their property taxes—"

"Commissioner Feilen, do you have any specific questions? If not—"

"I do, Madam Chair. I have a number of questions for the sheriff. Questions that should have been asked years ago, decades ago, before we tore down the budgetary walls for the road patrol. My first question, why do we give patrol officers a police cruiser for their private use?"

Ray looked directly at Feilen and held him in his gaze as he answered the question. "All officers in the law enforcement division are assigned a police vehicle. This is a common practice in regional police agencies. We are lightly staffed for the area we cover and the population we serve. We often have to call on off-duty officers to handle situations that require additional personnel. It only takes a few minutes for an officer to respond to a call when he has immediate access to a fully equipped police vehicle. Numerous studies have shown this practice to be cost effective. I would be happy to provide you with a bibliography of relevant research."

"I'm sure you would, Sheriff. I'm sure you would. If you look hard enough on the Internet you can find something that supports most anything. And this brings me to my next question. Lots of counties, especially in the U.P., have dropped their road patrols. Life seems to go on there. I'm not suggesting we go that far, but couldn't we reduce the road patrol, let the State Police pick up the slack?"

"Commissioner, if you look at our budget, you will see that part of our revenue comes from state sources. Most counties in Michigan provide 24/7 police services because county boards and their constituencies have decided to fund them."

"Are you done, Commissioner Feilen?"

"No, I'm just beginning."

"Would someone like to move the question?"

"Madam Chairperson, you can't just cut off debate—"

"Melvin, you would question every item on the budget if I gave you a chance. Like the sheriff tried to tell you, the services the department provides reflect political decisions made by this board over many, many decades. Your questions are not relevant to the budget items we are voting on. Will someone move the question?"

Ray listened to the roll call: six ayes, one nay.

After the final vote and the adjournment, as Ray made his way toward the exit, Charlotte Frederickson cut him off.

"Thank you for not feeding the horrid man. I would resign just to get away from him, but fortunately, he aspires to a higher office."

"Really," said Ray.

"Yes, he's eyeing a state senate seat. Word is he found some big-money backers. Don't say it. I know. God help us all. I'll let you go, Ray. I can see your mind is on more important things."

9

When Ray returned to his office, he found a folder on the otherwise empty surface of his desk with a yellow post-it note attached—Gillian Mouton Autopsy. Pulling the report from the folder, his eyes skipped down the page over the boilerplate until he reached *Immediate Cause of Death.* Then he slowed and read the section, carefully taking in every word and phrase.

Ray sat for a few moments and absorbed the information, and then he stood and hit a switch on the wall, lowering a large whiteboard. In the upper right hand corner he wrote, *Persons of Interest,* adding *Phillip Lovell* immediately below.

Sue rapped, than pushed open the door, "Dr. Dyskin was right on, strangulation, consistent with chokehold."

"You've become much more tolerant of the good doctor since he's given up cigars."

"I never questioned his expertise, I just couldn't tolerate the smell."

Sue glanced at the whiteboard. "I see you've started a list of people of interest," she said with a sardonic smile.

"Did Lovell show up to ID the body?"

"Yes."

"How did that go?"

"Lovell's facial expressions, his body language, the tone of his voice—all seemed authentic enough." She paused for a moment. "I'm probably reading into his reaction because of what we know about him, but I had this sense that his performance had been carefully rehearsed on his drive to the medical center. It was just too good.

"I started going through the address book on Gillian's Mac last night looking for possible next of kin. I found a Gregory Mouton. Guess where he lives?"

"I'm all ears," said Ray.

"Here in Cedar County."

"Related?"

"Yes, stepbrother, but Gillian didn't include that information. I went out to his house first thing this morning armed with our new death notification protocols. First, I established his relationship to Gillian, and then I delivered the sad news. I should mention that his wife, Sherry, was there, too. From that point, everything seemed to get very strange. There didn't seem to be much affection between the siblings. Both Gregory and his wife went out of their way to tell me they hadn't been in contact with Gillian for years. There were a lot of concerned looks back and forth. I really wanted to question them more aggressively, but given the circumstances, I held back. Anyway, we will want to talk to them again in the next day or two. Add them to the list. If nothing else, they may be able to provide some background on Gillian."

"Did they give you the names of other relatives?"

"Gregory didn't know of any."

"How about spouses or…?"

"Gregory said he heard she was once married and soon divorced. And then he made a sarcastic remark about how the guy was lucky to make an early escape."

"Did he give you a name or a time frame for the marriage?"

"No, he was pretty vague on that, but I can chase the info down."

"What else?" he asked.

"Gillian's remarkable attention to detail. For every listing in her address book, there's all the usual stuff: profession, phone numbers, addresses, e-mails, and websites. She also included the names of personal assistants, secretaries, spouses, ex-spouses, and significant others. Under attorney I found one listing, Stephanie Margolis,

J.D., New York City address. I called her when I got back to the office this morning. I had to fight my way past her very aggressive secretary. Margolis has a beautiful voice, like an opera singer. She was shocked by the news. Then she became wary, asking for my name and number. She called me back a few minutes later, after verifying that I was who I said I was.

"From that point forward Margolis was helpful. I asked about next of kin. Margolis stated that their relationship was mostly professional, but they did have an overlapping circle of friends. She couldn't help me with next of kin. She said she hadn't done any estate work for Gillian, and they had never talked about family. When I asked about possible love interests, Margolis said she didn't know much about that part of Gillian's life."

Sue looked down at her notes, then up at Ray. "There was one other local contact in her address book, a Geoffrey Fairfield."

"What about him?"

"He lives near the tip of East Bay about ten miles from where we found the body. I called and left a message. Do you know the name?"

Ray pondered her question for a long moment. "The name is sort of bouncing around in my head, but I don't think so. How about you?"

"No. I checked, he's not on our local radar. Make a new category, something like *Other People we need to talk to*. Fairfield will be one. Then there's Gillian's first husband, once I have a name and number."

"Gillian's relationship with Lovell—"

"More of an afternoon delight than a romance. Is that what you are trying to say, Ray?"

"Exactly. I wonder if she had someone else out there. Could this possibly be a crime of passion? Someone following her out here?"

"Don't know," said Sue. "The relationship item on her Facebook page reads: *It's complicated*. That probably doesn't mean anything. Most relationships are. I think that's what I would put on mine if I did Facebook."

Ray had sensed her current romance with a Chicago lawyer was starting to cool, but he thought it better not to ask. "Then there's the possibility of the secret admirer. Someone obsessed with her, someone she might not even have been aware of."

"A totally creepy character following her around. There's always that possibility, especially with such a public personality. Remember yesterday when Phillip Lovell said everyone in the wine industry knows Gillian Mouton?"

"Yes," Ray answered.

"Last night after I got done searching Gillian's contact list, I Googled her name again. The top hit, of course, was her website. It is so well done, and her personality really comes through. She was edgy, funny, smart, sarcastic, sexy and often outrageous. As well as her intended audience, I can see how she might have attracted some weird admirers."

Sue looked over at Ray. "Did you happen to check out her website, or were you trying to catch up on your *New Yorkers?*"

"I spent some time there," said Ray. "There was much to admire. A very professional site. She must have been a very interesting woman."

"So here's one possible angle," said Sue. "This wasn't a shoestring operation. Gillian had to be spending big bucks. I'm talking about all the high quality video, especially. I imagine she had to have a good cash flow to keep her business afloat."

"So you're wondering if there might be an economic angle to the crime?"

"A possibility, don't you think? For example, why the video of Lovell? Blackmail?"

"Blackmail? Who would he be trying to hide his dalliance with Gillian from, his married girlfriend?"

Sue gave Ray a slightly abashed smile. "I'm just trying to find a starting place."

"How about the car?" asked Ray.

"The car must have been detailed just before she picked it up. The only prints I could find were hers. Other than her personal things, there was one empty water bottle and the rental paperwork, that's it. " Sue tapped the closed cover of Mouton's laptop. "I need to spend some serious time looking through this and her phone. There's a mountain of data here: thousands of pictures, documents, e-mails, and text messages."

"Why don't you get started on that, and I'll run over and have a chat with Marty Donaldson. Maybe he can shed some light on why Gillian was in his vineyard in the middle of the night."

"Did you have some quality time with the county commission? Do we have a budget for the next fiscal year?"

"Yes. One dissenting vote. It was pretty much like I expected."

"Let me guess, Commissioner Feilen cast the dissenting vote?"

"Yes. He did some grandstanding along the way to a mostly empty room."

"What's the story on him?"

"I just know bits and pieces. He was three years ahead of me in school. Feilen was one of the school badasses. He enlisted at graduation and went off for a few years and grew up.

"His family had orchards from way back. His grandfather branched out into processing and canning. Feilen took over the family business after he returned from the service. I think things were already going south long before he took the helm.

"At some point he got tagged by the DEQ for contaminating a stream that runs through his property. Then he was sued by some of the farmers who lived downstream. Feilen ended up going bankrupt and was forced to liquidate most of his agricultural property. He was able to hold onto the old family farmstead, a gravel pit, and the buildings that once held the processing plant. I've heard he rents the building out for storage space and makes his living doing excavation work. We were all surprised when he managed to get elected to the county board."

"So you're off to talk to Marty Donaldson, and I'm going to see what more I can discover on Gillian's computer. Lunch?"

"It will have to be fast."

"Seems to be SOP."

10

Ray found Marty Donaldson operating a forklift behind the main winery building of Terroir Nord. He acknowledged Ray with a wave and continued with his task, picking up large yellow plastic bins filled with grapes and dumping the grapes into the top of a crusher, a massive piece of stainless steel machinery connected to numerous wires and hoses. Then he climbed off the forklift and worked at the control panel mounted to the frame of the crusher before joining Ray.

"Sorry for making you wait, Ray. No time to waste. We've got a lot of grapes to process today and more on the way for tomorrow."

"How're you doing?" asked Ray.

"I'm still in disbelief. I could hardly sleep last night. Got up and drove down there just to see that nothing was going on. Mary is on my back for repeatedly waking her up. Why me? Why here, Ray? What the hell is this all about? Have you identified that poor woman?"

"We have identified her. We're trying to find any next of kin before we go public with her name later today. The woman was Gillian Mouton."

"Really, Gillian Mouton."

"Did you know her?"

"Not personally, no. But in this industry, she was hard to miss. Her face is in all the wine magazines. She's at all the important trade shows."

"Other than Wednesday morning, did you ever see her in person?"

"I don't think so. How did she die? And why did she pick my vineyard?"

"We only have the most preliminary information from the autopsy. This was not a natural death, Marty."

"You're talking murder?"

"Yes." Ray let the information soak in, then asked, "She didn't show up in your tasting room in the last few days?"

"Not that I know of. Like I said, the wife and daughter-in-law mostly run that part of the business. The boys and I occasionally fill in. And we hire some college girls, too, during the busy season. I only look in occasionally. If they had seen her, I would have heard about it."

"Would they have known her by face?"

Donaldson looked thoughtful. "Good point. I'm sure they would have heard her name. Whether they would have recognized her in person, probably not."

Donaldson leaned against a steel column that supported the roof extending beyond the building. He looked out at the vine-covered trellises that ran along the undulating landscape. Turning back to Ray he asked, "You think she might have been in our tasting room?"

"I don't know that, Marty. I do know she was visiting area wineries."

"And how did her body end up in one of my vineyards?" he repeated.

"That's what we're trying to figure out."

"If she was murdered, like you say, maybe she was just dumped there."

"Marty, she was murdered where you found her body. That red Audi was hers, a rental. It appears she drove there alone. She must have been lured there by someone. We're trying to figure out the who and why."

"Ray, I have no idea. It's just a hill covered with grapevines like hundreds of others across the county. If someone was looking for a very remote place to do something like this, especially at night, that would be a good spot. Who the woman might have been meeting, obviously I couldn't even begin to speculate on."

"I'd like to talk to your wife."

"Mary's in the tasting room. You'll find my daughter-in-law there, too, unless she's off checking on the kids. I'll walk you over there."

"How about your sons?"

"You will have to catch them another day. They went down to Paw Paw to get a couple of truckloads of grapes we bought for one of our non-estate wines. They should be back sometime this evening."

11

Ray found Sue still working in his office when he returned. "Did you learn anything new from Donaldson?" she asked.

"He knew Gillian Mouton by reputation in the industry, but not by sight. Later I talked to his wife, daughter-in-law, and a couple of young women who work in the tasting room. I showed them a copy of the picture I pulled off Mouton's website. No one remembers seeing her in the tasting room. They did say they've been very busy with the color tour crowd. Lots of folks in and out. If she wasn't sampling at the tasting counter or didn't buy anything, they probably would have missed her."

"I've just started to work through her photos," said Sue. "I'm creating a time frame for Gillian starting with her arrival in Grand Rapids on Sunday. Her photos provide accurate times and locales. I think all of this material was intended to be content for her website. It appears that Gillian was working from a set format, probably more in her head than written down. Let me port these over to the big screen.

"As you can see, in every series she started with the winery sign at the road and then a distant shot of the tasting room. Then there's the panoramic pic of the vineyards and several more of the tasting room, both interior and exterior. The smiling owners show up in about half of the photo collections. My bet is that if they were handy, she got them, but meeting them was not her goal. Chatting them up would have taken too much time, and she was on a tight schedule. You probably remember seeing similar material when you looked at her website. I've gone through eight wineries so far and they follow the same plan."

"And the Ursidae Winery is represented in the same way?" asked Ray.

"Exactly, and not exactly."

"What's that supposed to mean?"

"Here's her quick tour of *Ursidae* from the file from Monday," she said. "The pics follow the same pattern as the others. And yes, Phillip Lovell was available for a mug shot, fortunately fully clothed. Then there's a second file labeled *Ursidae II*. These were shot Tuesday morning. Look at these. The photos in this collection do not follow the same pattern."

Ray studied the pictures very carefully as Sue moved through the series. "It appears she was part of a tour group, but her focus seems to be on the layout of the place and the security system. Looks like she might have been casing the place for a break-in."

"My thought, exactly. She probably signed up for the regular tour. Her camera was always pointed in the direction of something that would have been of normal interest to a shutter-happy tourist, but she was using a wide-angle lens so she was able to capture the things that she was really interested in."

"How did she pull this off?"

"Remember the jeans, hoodie, and hiking shoes in her trunk? I also found a baseball cap and some large sunglasses among her belongings. Probably her undercover clothes for just the Tuesday visit."

"So what was she after?" asked Ray. "Why this attention to security cameras?"

"She must have been considering an unchaperoned, after hours tour."

"Obviously, but why? What was she looking for?"

Ray mulled over Gillian's possible motives. "She obviously wasn't thinking of walking away with some wine. Trade secrets…in a winery…I don't think so. There is no secret formula like Coke or

Pepsi. It's wine—grape juice, some yeast, perhaps a little extra sugar, and a skillful winemaker."

"Was she trying to get something on Lovell?" said Sue.

"What and why? We've speculated on blackmail as the motive for the condo video. But that doesn't seem to work…sex between consenting adults."

"Speaking of that, we need to talk to Lovell's alibi, Olivia Jakmond. That's got to happen tomorrow."

Ray's mind was racing. "How thoroughly did you look at her website? Is there any evidence that she did exposés, yellow journalism?"

"There's so much there, but my impression is that Gillian was a cheerleader for the industry. Yes, there's an edgy quality to her writing, but her focus was on drawing attention to quality affordable wines, often from new, small, and unknown producers. She occasionally ridiculed a wine with funny things like tasting notes of 'cheap cigars, watermelon flavored bubblegum, and Old Spice stick deodorant.' But her negative reviews were few and far between."

"How about e-mail, social media, and cell calls?"

"Just getting started, Ray. She doesn't seem to have a Twitter account, that's surprising. On Facebook she did the bare minimum to keep a presence. Working through her mail and messages is going to take days, maybe even weeks. There is so much there."

"We know she was casing Ursidae. If we could only figure out what she was looking for. I wish we could get a look at their security video from the time she was in the winery. Perhaps that would provide a useful clue or two."

"And what if she was recognized? Her snooping might have gotten her killed." She looked over at Ray. "Where do we go from here?"

"Press conference in fifteen minutes. Tomorrow morning we start with Gillian's stepbrother, and then we check out Lovell's alibi. What's her name again?"

"Olivia Jakmond. I've got a phone number and e-mail. She's a realtor, young and blond, at least in her pictures. I'll try to set up both of those interviews before I leave. And then we should see if we can find this Fairfield character."

12

Gregory Mouton, Gillian's stepbrother, met Ray and Sue at the screen door on his front porch. "I think we'll be a lot more comfortable on the deck. We'll get the early morning sun there," he said. He led them through the living room and dining room to the back of the century old structure.

Ray glanced at Mouton as he settled into one of the four Adirondack chairs. Mouton appeared to be in his 50s. He was mostly bald, his polo shirt ballooned over his beltline.

"This is my wife, Sherry," said Mouton as a small blond woman came out of the house carrying a tray with cups and a coffee carafe. She departed as soon as the coffee was served.

"It would be best if your wife joined us," said Ray.

"Is that really necessary, Sheriff? I think she'd prefer not to be part of the conversation. She's very upset by Gillian's death."

"Please ask her to join us."

Ray watched Mouton pull his bulk out of the sloping chair and go back into the house. They waited in silence, listening to the muted conversation from within. Several minutes later Mouton returned, his wife following him.

Ray stood and motioned Sherry Mouton toward one of the center chairs and indicated to Gregory that he should sit next to her. Then he dragged his chair around so he could look directly at the pair. Sue followed suit.

"Thank you for agreeing to see us this morning. When Sergeant Lawrence notified you of Gillian Mouton's passing yesterday, we were still dealing with an unexplained death. Since that time we have determined that she was murdered. We were hoping that you might be able to provide us more information about your stepsister."

After a long silence, Gregory began, "Like I told your sergeant yesterday, we've been estranged from Gillian for years. We just don't know anything about her."

"Why weren't you and your stepsister talking?"

"She dropped us long ago," said Sherry. "Gillian was a user, and we didn't have anything left to give."

"I asked your husband the question. I need his answer."

Gregory looked over at his wife and then focused on Ray. "There are years of history, lots of blood under the dam. I'll give you the condensed version, Sheriff. As you know, Gillian was a stepsister, not a sister. She was part of the baggage that came along when my dad hooked up with Bonnie, Gillian's mother. After they were married, Bonnie made sure my father adopted Gillian. At that time she took our family name. I think she was a bastard child, never heard anything about her biological father. My dad made good on his obligation to Gillian, even though Bonnie had wandered off with someone else by then. He supported her through college. And then she disappeared from his life. We were all shocked when she showed up for his memorial service. I don't know how she knew about it. I'm sure she was just there to stake her claim to part of the estate. Dad always said he was going to write her out, but he didn't."

"Gillian didn't do a damn thing for him ever, not a thing," said Sherry. "We took care of Mike for years. And as soon as he passed, the bitch is right there demanding her share. This is all we've got left, Sheriff, all we've got left. Just this old, crumbling farmhouse and a few acres of knapweed. And we almost had to sell it to generate the cash to settle the estate."

"This house has been in the family for years," said Gregory. "It was our up north place. My grandfather bought it sometime in the 50s." Mouton looked over the top of his glasses and made a sweeping gesture with his hand. "This property was once part of a much larger parcel that ran all the way down to the water. After we made the permanent move north, we started selling off parcels to stay afloat. Dad was living with us then. There were lots of expenses."

"When was that?" asked Ray.

"We made a permanent move in 2008. Before that we lived in Birmingham. My father had a very successful tool and die shop in Royal Oak. After college I started working in the business. Then it all went away. Death by a thousand cuts. The auto industry has been dying for, what, forty years. My dad always said the 1973 oil crisis was the beginning of the end. The big three could never figure out that the world was changing. We held on by our fingernails from one crisis to the next for years. But this last recession, that was the doomsday. We just couldn't survive anymore.

"So here I am, almost fifty years old, and this is what I own." He gestured with his hand to indicate the house and surrounding property. "And I had to fight with Gillian to keep this. She demanded half the value."

"Was the estate settled here or downstate?"

"Downstate, Oakland County. My father's lawyer, Theodore Weisz, looked after things. The man has got to be close to ninety, but he's still sharp as nails."

"Where's he located?"

"Birmingham, on old Woodward. He's probably been in the same office for 50 years."

"Tell me about your history with Gillian. Start at the beginning."

"I was in college when my father married Gillian's mother, Bonnie. My parents had divorced when I left for college. I think they had done their best to stay together till then. I don't think they liked each other for a very long time. My mother quickly married the golf pro at the country club. They moved to Arizona.

"Bonnie had been a clerical in the company office. Not long after the divorce, she and my father became an item. I didn't dream he'd marry her. She wasn't a lot older than me, something like thirty years younger than Dad. What did I know? It was only a matter of months.

"My father and Bonnie stayed together for a while, and I think had some good years. Eventually the difference in their ages became a problem. I don't think Gillian spent much time with my dad after the divorce. Gillian was in college by then and only came around when she wanted something, mainly money. But she knew how to work him, just like Bonnie."

"And your relationship with Gillian?"

"At the beginning of their marriage it was really good. I mean, I suddenly had this cute little seven or eight-year-old sister. I was an only child. I always wanted a brother or sister. I finally got one, albeit rather late. And she just seemed to adore me. We'd come up here for vacations, summer and winter. I taught Gillian how to water-ski, downhill ski, and how to handle a sailboat. She was a real jock, had this joyful laugh. I was out of school by then, working and dating. I think my dad and Bonnie were together about ten years. The divorce was all about money. Bonnie ended up with half of his net worth.

"We lost the business in 2008 as GM, our major customer, slid toward bankruptcy. I was running the company by then. Dad was still coming in every day. There were just a few of us left—Dad, me, and a couple of old-timers who had been with us for decades. Dad and I both had houses in Birmingham. We sold them off in a soft market and moved up here.

"My wife and I, we're pretty much taking care of Dad by then. During those years we never heard from Gillian. Not once, not even a phone call or a card. Then Dad started to really deteriorate, a series of small strokes and a big one finally that killed him. And during this time he kept saying, 'I need to get this land out of the estate and into your name.' But it never happened. So after he passed I had to dip into our limited assets to buy Gillian out so we could continue to live here. I told Gillian that my dad had wanted for me to have the place. We had been his caregivers for years. She treated it like a joke. I was going to contest the will, but my lawyer said it would just be throwing good money after bad."

"And that's the last contact you had with Gillian?" asked Ray, watching Mouton closely.

"Like I told your sergeant here."

"Yes, I know what you told her. Is that the complete truth?"

A long silence followed. "You should see the sunrise from here. Just spectacular. I keep telling the wife, we may be hanging on by our nails, but we're still a couple of the luckiest people on the planet."

"Did you see Gillian again?" asked Sue.

"Well, what you have to understand is there are two Gillians, the good Gillian and the bad Gillian. The good Gillian was one of most charming people you'd ever want to meet—warm, engaging, funny, and very pretty. The other Gillian, the bad Gillian, was a self-serving bitch. So…"

"Don't go there," said Sherry.

"This is a murder investigation," said Ray. "Withholding information constitutes obstruction of justice. When did you last see Gillian?"

"I knew she was going to be in the area. There was a big article about her wine event in the *Northern Express*."

"My question, Gregory, when did you last see Gillian Mouton?"

He remained silent, looking off at the horizon. "She was here on Sunday," he finally said. "The good Gillian. She just came up the drive Sunday like nothing had ever happened between us. First she carries in a case of wine, high-end French stuff, names I didn't know. Then she goes back to the car for another box of fancy cheeses and crackers. Hundreds of dollars worth of stuff. She called it a peace offering. I'm embarrassed to admit that I was totally sucked in. The good Gillian had me right back playing big brother, little sister.

"We opened a bottle of wine or two and worked our way through some of the cheese. Then she asks me if I still had the boat." Mouton, who had been staring off toward the east, looked over at Ray, then at Sue. "It's a wooden boat, an old Chris Craft runabout. My grandfather bought it sometime in the 50s. My dad and I restored it before he died. That was our last project together. Anyway, back in happier times, I'd take Gillian for cruises. Her favorite trip was up around the top of the bay and then down to Sleeping Bear Dunes. We'd anchor offshore, swim in, and climb the tallest dune. You know the big lake. We had to do it on days there was quiet water. Remember Sunday, absolutely flat. I was an easy mark."

"So you went to Sleeping Bear Dunes and back."

"Yes, but we didn't make the climb, stayed in the boat. She was more into taking photos. I figured out later she had another agenda that had nothing to do with me."

"And that was?" asked Sue.

"She wanted to get some vineyard shots from the water. She was really fixated on one of the vineyards, but the angles were all wrong she said. And it's real steep there. There's a deck on the tasting room that extends out over the ridgeline. She asked me if it would be a difficult climb."

"Do you remember which winery?" asked Sue.

"No, I don't think it was ever mentioned."

"Would it have been a difficult climb?" asked Ray.

"Well, technically no, especially if you're sixteen or seventeen and very fit. You know the area on the northwest shore of the peninsula. There are some really high, steep dunes there. There's lots of sand and heavy brush. Not an impossible climb, but it would take some scrambling. Not something that I would undertake anymore." He patted his gut as he looked over at Ray.

"Any idea of why she was interested in that winery?"

"Sheriff, I was wondering that, too. I asked her, but didn't get much of an answer. As soon as we got back and had the boat tied up, she was off. A quick hug and she was gone. And then it hit me. The wine, the goodies, all the charm and happy talk had one purpose. She needed both me and the boat. We were just part of a larger plan. I don't know what this was all about. I guess you will figure it out."

"Could you tell us the area that Gillian seemed to be interested in?" asked Sue.

"No problem. I'll need a map."

Sue retrieved a map from her Jeep, and they moved to the kitchen and gathered around the table. Ray and Sue held the corners to keep the map flat.

"Once we cleared the top of the peninsula, our course was sort of a straight line down to the dunes. Coming back, Gillian asked me if I would stay closer in. I held a course about two hundred yards off shore." Using his finger as a pointer, he said, "There were several areas where vineyards are visible, and she was snapping away, but this area seemed to be her main focus."

"Did you see Gillian again, after she got off your boat?"

"No. Didn't expect I ever would."

"And you had no further communication with her—phone, text, e-mail?"

"No. None."

"Wednesday evening, where were you?" asked Sue.

"Let me think, Wednesday, we had a late dinner at the casino. Then we came home. It must have been at least ten-thirty, maybe close to eleven. I crawled into bed with a book."

"Is there anyone who can vouch for your presence at the casino?"

"The wait staff, the bartender, we're on a first name basis. And I used a credit card."

Sue started the engine. "What do you think?"

"We need to check Gregory's alibi. If you believe his story, Gillian skillfully manipulated him for her photographic tour. Could she have manipulated him to meet her at the vineyard for help on another excursion? It's not a tight alibi."

"How about Sherry? There's a lot of anger there. The settling of estates often tears families apart. "

"And if you buy into her version of things," said Ray, "it's easy to understand Sherry's anger. Sherry would have needed a gun. She's too small, too slight to overpower Gillian."

"What do you think," said Ray, "ten years difference between the two of them?"

"Maybe not that much. But he's running to fat, and she looks like she's taking care of herself."

"The lawyer Mouton mentioned, Theodore Weisz, give him a call. Tell him about Gillian's murder and see what you can find out about the estate."

"Will do. As I drive, look over the material I collected on Olivia Jakmond. There's a photo, too, after the last page. She looks like a real piece of work. She and Lovell probably deserve one another."

13

Ray worked his way through Olivia Jakmond's dossier: marriages and divorces, bankruptcies, and lawsuits. There was also a list of recent traffic violations, most involving speeding. Then he flipped to the last page. A very blond woman, blond eyebrows, too, with pinkish skin and pale blue eyes stared back at him.

Sue glanced over to see if he was still reading. "What do you think?"

"She looks quite benign, but she seems to leave a hell of a lot of wreckage in her wake. These legal problems, did you get any sense of the reasons for suits?"

"Politely stated, different interpretations of the terms of a contract. Less politely, she's a dirty, lying…well, you can fill in the blanks."

"Well, just the kind of person we need to make an alibi credible. Where are we meeting her?"

"West Bay Towers, Penthouse Level, 'Traverse City's most exclusive condominium address'. I think that's the way the advert on her website reads."

As the glass-sided elevator started its ascent, Sue said, "I could get used to this."

Ray chuckled, "Your pay doesn't buy this view of the bay."

"Nor yours."

"Any idea what these places cost?"

"A million five on the penthouse level. The place is a steal, marked down from two-point-two. The rooftop patio with sauna and two private parking spaces are included. There is, however, an upcharge for a yacht slip."

"What a deal," said Ray, as the doors opened to a hallway.

"We're looking for 9-A," said Sue, leading the way.

They found the door of 9-A ajar. Sue knocked, and then pushed it open. They could see a woman on the balcony, her back to them, teetering on spike heels, holding a cell phone to her ear with one hand. In her other hand, stretched out over the balcony, she held a cigarette. Ray watched her take a final puff, then flick the cigarette away.

"Quite the joint," said Sue, under her breath as she looked around.

Olivia Jakmond turned in their direction and gave a quick wave before briefly returning to her conversation. A few moments later she pushed open the door and joined them.

"Sorry for that. Rude of me. I was just putting the finishing touches on an important deal." After inspecting their IDs, she extended a hand, first to Sue, then to Ray. "And thank you for coming here. The office wouldn't be a good place for this conversation. Please have a seat," she said motioning toward a counter area with tall stools. "I've just made some coffee."

Ray looked closely at Jakmond as she was pouring the coffee. She appeared to be fifteen or twenty years older than the woman in the photo Sue copied from her website.

"This is a lovely condo," Sue said.

"It is, isn't it. I've been involved with this project from the beginning. This unit, this condo, is my baby. Everything, the decorating, the layout. It's turnkey. Sheets on the beds, towels in the baths, everything is here but the new owner's toothbrush."

"So it hasn't been sold yet?" asked Ray.

"No, but it will. We've been close a couple of times, trouble with the financing. The place is a steal. You'd pay three times the asking price if this were in the Hamptons or Cape Cod. And with direct flights from Newark, you get here faster."

Jakmond's sales-pitch smile faded. "Let's get this over with, shall we?"

"We need to verify that you were with Phillip Lovell on Wednesday evening," said Ray.

"What's going to happen with what I tell you? It's not going to be in the paper or—"

"Ms. Jakmond, this is a murder investigation. It's very important that you tell us the truth." Ray waited for her response.

"It's a bit clumsy. My husband and I are separating, it just hasn't happened yet. And Phillip and I sort of got involved. You see my husband is a corporate pilot, he's gone a lot and my hooking up with someone else could complicate the divorce."

"We just need to know about Wednesday evening."

"And that murder, it's just so sad. A young, beautiful woman. Certainly Phillip couldn't be involved in anything like that."

"Were you with him on Wednesday evening? If so, what time did he arrive? When did he leave? Were you with him the whole time? That's the information we need," said Ray.

"Yes, I was with him. Things weren't very good."

"Where?"

"Here. There are only two units on this level. They are both empty. It's a very discrete place to meet someone."

As Ray watched, Jakmond, sitting on the other side of the counter, turned away and gazed out at the lake. Then she turned in his direction. She looked tired and frightened.

"We were supposed to have dinner here, he was going to spend the night. He was going to meet me at 6:00. He finally called, but it was long after he should have been here. It went to my voicemail. I was talking to someone else. His message was that he had to spend time with a client and something to the effect that he knew I would understand. Why do men do that when they're pulling some shit? 'I know you will understand.' I was pissed. I had planned a perfect evening. I had all of his favorite things from Red Ginger."

"I didn't know they did takeout," said Sue.

"They don't," said Jakmond emphatically. "He got here sometime after nine. I had purchased a very special bottle of champagne, and I had consumed more than I should have before he got here. I was royally pissed, and I wanted him to know how angry I was. I have a husband who has pulled this kind of shit for years. I'm not going to let anyone else do this to me."

"You said he finally arrived sometime after nine, Ms. Jakmond?" Ray pressed. "What time, exactly?"

"I'm not sure, to tell you the truth. By then I had had quite a bit of champagne."

"To the best of your ability, give us a chronology of what happened."

"We were arguing. Finally, I calmed down a bit. You know, he can be quite charming. We finished off the champagne, and I opened a backup bottle, not as good as the first one, but good enough. We sort of made up and went to bed, not that anything wonderful happened. We'd both had way too much to drink."

"So you were together all night?"

"Yes."

"Till what time?" asked Sue.

"Phillip was up early, before 6:00. I offered to make him some coffee, but he said he'd just pick some up on his way back out to the winery. I was out of here before seven. Went home to shower and get some fresh clothes."

"Have you talked to Mr. Lovell since?"

"Yes, he called me yesterday. Said I should expect to hear from you. To be quite frank, I was totally pissed that he gave you my name. So much for defending the good name of a woman."

"What you've just told us, is that completely accurate, or did Lovell coach you a bit?" pressed Ray.

"That's exactly what happened. The man's on his own. I will do nothing to save his sorry ass."

"I noticed that you have security cameras throughout the public areas of this building. Is there a way we could verify what you've told us by viewing the video from that time period?" asked Sue.

Jakmond was slow to respond. "I don't know how we can do that. I mean it wouldn't look good. It might get me fired. I'm sure if the owners knew…."

"This is a murder investigation. We'd have no trouble getting a search warrant."

"I'll see what I can do," said Jakmond. "Give me a few days."

A few minutes later, as Sue headed north on 22, Ray asked, "Was she telling us the truth?"

"Mostly. We had her in a box. She knew that we would have seen the cameras. Now she's sweating about how she's going to get us the video without getting fired in the process. She's not going to have a good weekend."

"Keep the pressure on for those videos. Not that it would completely absolve him from being involved, but at least we would know Lovell didn't do the killing."

14

Sue maneuvered her Jeep along the curvy coastal road as Ray looked through the notes she had gathered on Geoffrey Fairfield, the name of an area resident found on Gillian's contact list.

"Not much on Fairfield."

"No, there wasn't much there: a list of old addresses, he divorced a few years ago, some notices on his business as an independent insurance investigator. He doesn't use social media, and his website, one page only, has little more than contact information.

"And he was one of the missing persons for a high school reunion. Did you show up for yours, Ray?"

"Seldom. What's the first one, five years? I was living in Europe. Later I was building a life and a career. I was always nostalgic about this place, people included, but I didn't care much about reunions. How about you?"

"My ten year is still in the future."

"Pull off here. I want to walk on the shore a bit. We're not late, are we?"

"For once, we're running ahead of time."

Ray climbed out of the Jeep and walked to shore. Settling on a grassy knoll, he peered across the gently rolling water to the other side of the bay. As he sat quietly taking in the scene, he reviewed the events of the last few days. So many images floated through his consciousness. Finally, he pulled himself to his feet and rejoined Sue.

"What's going on," she asked.

"I need to slow things down. High heels?"

"Yes."

"I imagine Gillian…I don't know quite how to say it…I imagine she looked good walking with them on."

"I would think. She was tall, thin, and elegant—the type of woman who wears them well."

"And Olivia Jakmond, she couldn't do it at all. She seemed off balance."

"Some women don't look right in heels, Ray, not that it prevents them from wearing them."

"But why, that's what I'm interested in."

"Maybe it's age. She's got to be pushing fifty. Or maybe the bones in her feet are already damaged from too many years of stiletto abuse. And she's carrying some extra weight in her hips; it might be about physics. Is that what you were thinking about out there? I thought you were having a Thoreauian moment," she said before pulling onto the highway.

"Nice piece of land," said Sue as she rolled to a stop at the end of a long macadam drive. Beyond the neatly kept Victorian cottage, Ray could see an elaborate seawall, the big lake stretching beyond.

Geoffrey Fairfield—tall, blond, in a blue button-down shirt, khakis, and loafers—was on the front porch to greet them before the vehicle stopped. He guided them into the interior, serving coffee around a sturdy oak kitchen table.

"I saw the story of Gillian's death on the news last night. I was just shocked. In truth, I was only half listening. I immediately went to the station's website just to make sure it was really Gillian."

Geoffrey Fairfield looked at Sue, "How did you get my name?"

"Gillian Mouton's address book. I was looking for local contacts. How did you know her?"

"It goes back a lot of years. During high school I worked as a mechanic in the local ski shop in downtown Birmingham. We weren't really mechanics, but that's the title they gave us," he explained. "I mounted and tested bindings, sharpened edges, did wax jobs, that kind of thing. Gillian, she was a couple of years younger than me. She was on her school's ski team. She went to Cranbrook. I went to Seaholm, the public school. She'd come in to the shop on a regular basis, usually with her mother, occasionally with her stepdad. He was a lot older than her mother. Nice man, though. Once I got to know him, he always wanted my advice on the equipment Gillian should be skiing. He was a good customer. Had some big bucks. Never really asked the price of anything.

"Gillian, she had three or four pairs of skis, high-end models, always wanted them perfect for racing. She was really cute. It was fun chatting her up."

Ray, listening, looked around the room. The place looked like a period cottage, going back many generations.

"I would see her skiing, mostly the local places around Detroit, Mt. Brighton, Holly, Alpine Valley. Maybe once at Boyne or the Highlands. Sometimes we'd hang out together on the slopes, and we went on a few dates.

"Birmingham, it's an interesting place. The town is divided by a major thoroughfare, Woodward Avenue. Most of the affluence is west of Woodward. It's divided a second time by 15 Mile Road. The southeast corner of the city is the least affluent part—small houses, mostly frame, a few brick that date from just after WWII. That's where I lived. I had hardworking parents with low-paying jobs. Me and my four siblings were packed into a nine-hundred foot, two-floor bungalow. Gillian was from the other side of the great divide, same with all her friends. You know how teenagers are, I would never have shown her where I lived.

"Her mother was very protective, and I could tell she didn't think I measured up. The few times we went out, she needed to know where we were every moment. I always had the sense that she was following us. Like I said, we had a couple dates, that was it. Her stepfather was a nice guy. He continued to come into the ski shop as long as I worked there. Always asked for me. Didn't want anyone else to work on his skis."

"So you didn't see Gillian after that?" asked Sue.

"I saw her around town a few times and then didn't run into her again for years."

"Where was that?"

"Ann Arbor. After high school I continued to work at the ski shop. I went to the community college, which I hated. All my friends had gone away to school. One noon I talked to a marine recruiter in the cafeteria. The military offered me a way out, and I took it. I stayed in five years, did a couple of tours in Iraq.

"When I got back, I enrolled at Michigan. I was in business administration. I ran into Gillian in the business school library one day. I hardly recognized her. There I was, a sophomore, and she was in her final year of an MBA program. The cute teenager had turned into an incredibly sophisticated woman. I could tell she was way out of my league.

"We caught a coffee at the little Italian joint right across the street. Gillian was married then, had a really big rock. Told me she met the guy at Vail, a trust fund baby who'd moved to town while she finished her degree. I met him once. She'd invited me to a holiday party. Nice guy, graying at the temples, probably early forties, a sugar daddy of sorts. After that semester, I lost touch with her."

"How did your name and number end up in her address book?" asked Sue.

"When her stepdad died, I saw his obituary in the *Record Eagle*. He had always been first class to me. I went to the memorial service. I guess in the back of my mind was the possibility that she'd be there. She was. We caught a drink after at the Park Place. The conversation was mainly about her, the wine business, the blog, all that stuff.

"She wasn't wearing the big diamond anymore. I asked about her husband. She told me that was long over. They weren't growing in the same direction. Then she asked me to run her to the airport. Before we said goodbye, she asked for my phone number, gave me hers. It was one of those moments where you know the woman will never call, but you go through the paces. It just seems to be the thing to do. That was it."

"No further contact?"

"Never."

"Did you know she was going to be in the area this week."

"Yes, I saw an advertisement for her event."

"But you weren't interested in…?"

"Sometimes you just need to let the past go. You know what I mean. We live in different worlds."

"What do you do, sir?" asked Ray.

"I'm an independent insurance investigator. I have my own business. Even as a high school student, I always wanted to live up here. After college I worked around Detroit for lots of years. I was always trying to figure out how to move up here. I found this place about the time the market bottomed out. It was part of an estate, and the sellers were eager to unload it. I made a ridiculous bid, and they took it. I've had to scramble to make a living, but it's worked out. I'm not rich, but I'm keeping a roof over my head."

"Where were you Wednesday evening?"

His demeanor suddenly changed, and there was an edge to his tone. "Why would you even be interested in where I was? I don't even know Gillian anymore. She's like a ghost from the past."

"It's just a routine question, sir," interjected Sue. "We're talking to everyone in the area who had any knowledge of Gillian Mouton. The question is just part of our normal procedure."

"I was here, alone."

"And you were here all evening?" Sue continued.

"Like I said, I was here all night. I may have run up to the Spartan store for cigarettes and a six-pack. I'm not sure if that was Tuesday or Wednesday. You know how days blend."

Sue handed Fairfield a business card. "We're still trying to get a handle on who this woman was. If you think of anything that might help us, please call. We'd appreciate your input."

On their way out, Ray stopped to inspect a wine rack at the end of a counter. "It looks like you're quite interested in wine, Mr. Fairfield."

"Yes, it's been a hobby since I was in the military. I was stationed in Europe."

"And you enjoy reds, French reds?"

"Yes, it's all about terroir, you know. Our local reds are getting drinkable, but you can never quite duplicate the land."

Back in Sue's Jeep, Ray asked, "What do you think?"

"He's sort of cute. Too bad he smokes."

"I didn't know you were looking," said Ray.

"I'm not, but things sometimes change. That flash of anger was interesting. You hit something, Ray. Maybe he just doesn't like cops."

"I wonder if there was any recent contact between them."

"Not that he's admitting to. I didn't find anything recent on Gillian's phone. Of course, she might have deleted calls or messages. Who knows what we'll find when I get the complete records from the phone company. I loved his comment about keeping a roof over his head. Quite a roof, isn't it. What do you think that place cost?"

"Beautiful location, lakefront. Plenty. Although most people would tear that Victorian down and put a trophy home on a lot like that."

"That's what I was thinking, too. What do you think it's worth?"

"At least a million for the lot. The beautiful old cottage was just a bonus. He must have found a good line of work. We know he didn't inherit anything."

"How about the wine?"

"I could only see the bottles at the top. They were all high-end burgundies. Maybe they were positioned for show while the rest of the rack was filled with something more pedestrian. Anyway, it looks like Mr. Fairfield has plenty of disposable income."

15

"Did you read the autopsy report yet?" Ray asked Sue as she came into his office later that morning. "There's also an appended note from Dr. Dyskin on the time of death."

"I just completed looking through it a few minutes ago. The 10:00 approximate time of death seems to fit with what we already know. Gillian was with Lovell until close to 9:00. It would have taken her 30 to 40 minutes to drive to the vineyard. She might have walked around town for a few minutes before she went to her car. Anyway, it works."

"So what does that tell us about the killer?" Ray asked.

"This was a planned killing," said Sue, "murder with premeditation. How was her killer able to lure her to a very isolated location?"

"That's what I don't understand. What possible enticement could someone offer to get her there? It was dark, getting cool. And this woman was no fool."

Sue opened her laptop, waited a bit, and made a series of entries. "Not much light Wednesday night. New moon. And if there was cloud cover, I'd have to find out how extensive the cloud cover was. Maybe they had a flashlight, but I bet the perp was navigating by ambient light." She paused for an instant. "Here's a scenario. They pull in and park. Maybe the perp stops and opens the gate, then waves her in and follows. They stand outside their cars as the perp waits for his eyes to adjust to the darkness. Then they move away from her car a bit. The perp swings behind her, effectively cuts off the blood flow to her brain, and in a minute or two drops her lifeless body and leaves the scene. And instead of going back up to the main road, he heads west on the two-track and doesn't even need to turn on his headlights till he hits the pavement again."

"That's good," he said, handing her a marker.

Sue started a column:

Perp:

- knows the area

- killing skills

- some acquaintance with Gillian or some powerful enticement

"Lovell and Fairfield know the area," said Sue. "And it wouldn't be hard for her stepbrother to figure it out. The killing skills, sophisticated, something that might have been learned in the military or martial arts. Geoffrey Fairfield was a marine. Gregory Mouton is certainly big enough and strong enough. Phillip Lovell—I can't imagine him having the strength of body or purpose to overpower anyone, especially after seeing that video. But actually going through with it, killing up close, that takes a certain kind of person or tremendous rage."

"At this point, we have no evidence that suggests that this could have been a crime of passion. We know almost nothing about her personal life. I wonder if she might have had a best friend to whom she divulged—"

"When I talk to her lawyer again, I'll ask about friends. But I'm not sure we would learn anything, even if we were able to run down some of her friends. Ray, I don't share that kind of information with my women friends. And Gillian was a professional woman who traveled a lot. She probably wouldn't have the time or inclination for that kind of conversation. Gillian was a very attractive woman and public personality. I'm sure she attracted her share of admirers. How about some weirdo with a rich fantasy life?"

"That's one of the possibilities we can't dismiss. But what if this is about money. She was looking for something and had an inordinate interest in Ursidae Winery. Phillip Lovell doesn't seem to be a hardened killer. But he could hire an assassin with an ample bag of tricks. The chokehold is quick. There's no noise, no bullet casing to find in the dark, no blood on his person, no weapon to dispose of. He simply does the job and drives away."

"Motive for Lovell?"

"I wish we had one."

"Running with your idea, let's say it was someone other than Lovell who wanted to make her go away, what kind of threat might Gillian have posed? There's so much more to learn. I did some background research last night."

"I thought you were going to yoga with the women?"

"I did. But my mind was on the case. I skipped the bar after."

"What did you learn?" asked Ray.

"No felony charges against Gregory Mouton, Geoffrey Fairfield, or Phillip Lovell. Phillip Lovell has an extensive bio on the Ursidae website. It looks padded to me, but I didn't have time to check it out. I'm curious to see if he has all the degrees and certifications that are listed there.

"For me, the more interesting thing was the background on the company that owns Ursidae, Seven Continent Spirits and Wine, LLC. As near as I can see, they have operations world-wide. It appears that they were once mostly a distributor, a middleman between producers and wholesalers. In the last decade they've start acquiring distilleries in the UK, Finland, and Greece. Ursidae is their first winery."

"I can see how they could be making the local producers uncomfortable," said Ray. "A multinational company—a Walmart or Amazon—moves to town and has the resources to change the game. If I were a local, I would be uncomfortable."

After a long silence, he asked, "Did you spend any more time on Gillian's computer or phone?"

"Just surface stuff, Ray. Nothing is jumping out yet. The interesting thing is that the perp didn't take her phone. People's lives are on these devices. The perp knew the phone contained no incriminating evidence. I will spend more time this weekend with her phone, iPad, and computer, but I'm not optimistic about some major breakthrough."

"I thought we had this pact about getting a life and not working through the weekend. No visitor from Chicago?"

"No, we're taking some time off. Stepping back a bit to think about things." She looked at Ray. "Paddling below Ursidae Winery today or tomorrow?"

"Probably paddling, but not there. Even if we had complete access to the place, we wouldn't know what we were looking for even if we stumbled over it."

16

Hanna Jeffers rolled into a parking space facing Lake Michigan. "Should we bother unloading the kayaks?" she asked Ray as they peered out at the pounding surf. They had met earlier in the year at the regional medical center while Ray was recuperating from injuries sustained while responding to a 911 call. At the time, Hanna was still struggling with post-traumatic stress disorder, the aftereffects of a tour as a combat surgeon. Ray and Hanna were drawn together by their addiction to big-water kayaking.

"Let's walk down and see how bad it is," said Ray.

They scrambled over a low dune and walked down to the high-water point. In the distance they could see large waves being propelled by the strong southwesterly winds, their dark gray crests outlined against the horizon. Closer to shore, the waves began breaking at the first sandbar fifty or more yards out, then building in amplitude as they broke with greater force as they approached the shore.

"We'd be broached before we ever launched," yelled Hanna over the sound of the wind and waves.

Ray nodded his head in assent. "It's wild out there. This is a good afternoon to hike on the beach."

"Too much sand blowing around," she pointed toward her eyes. "Contacts."

Hand in hand they walked back to the car. As she snapped on the seatbelt, Hanna said, "The wind is from the south southwest. We can just go up the shore a few miles and launch in the lee of

Sleeping Bear Point and paddle in protected water. Maybe we could even venture out beyond the point and play in the bumps for a bit. I need to be in a boat. I'm about to explode."

"You've just done a 180, Hanna. We could paddle on one of the smaller inland lakes," said Ray. "We haven't done that much. There are lots of places I'd like to show you."

"Consistency is not one of my virtues. Big water is my drug of choice. I lose control when I get near it. This is where I need to be," she responded emphatically, pointing out at the rolling surf. Then she backed out and down the access road, turning north when she hit the highway.

Thirty minutes later, clad in drysuits and helmets, they carried their kayaks to the beach, positioning the bows well beyond the water's edge. Hanna slid into her boat and attached her spray skirt. Ray pushed her out into the gentle swells, and then launched his kayak. Hanna did a few practice rolls as she waited for him to catch up.

Ray pulled to her side and reached over to hold on to her boat. "What do you think?" he asked, looking toward the rolling waves beyond the protection of the headland.

"Wouldn't want to lose a boat in this wind. We'd never catch it again," she said. While Ray was still rafted with her, Hanna pulled her towrope from the nylon bag at her waist and attached the carabineer to a strap on her PFD, in easy reach for deployment. Ray followed suit.

"Ready?" she yelled over the roar of the wind.

Ray nodded and carefully gripped his paddle as he released her boat. They paddled into the wind, the wind and waves building as they moved beyond the protection of the headland. Ray focused on keeping his bow perpendicular to the incoming waves. Their progress into deeper water was slow and labored as they confronted the tall waves and high wind, Ray often losing sight of Hanna in the surging water.

The big waves came in sets, lulls in between. As his bow started to climb with each new wave, he paddled hard to keep forward momentum. His bow suddenly buried in a wave before reaching the crest, the oncoming wall of water slamming into his chest, driving his torso back onto the rear deck. He recovered just in time to prepare for the next wave. This time he speared the crest of the wave with his broad paddle blade, bisecting the swell before it hit him.

During a brief lull, he looked for Hanna. Catching a glimpse of her, he gestured toward shore as his bow began to rise again. The first wave in the set was steep and powerful, foam being blown off the crest by the howling wind. After breaking through the top, he slipped into the trough and positioned his boat for the next whitecap. This one appeared to be much steeper than the last, towering over him as his bow began to rise. Ray paddled furiously toward the crest, moving the broad carbon blade quickly from side to side, grabbing as much water as possible with each stroke. As he neared the apex of the wave, he could feel the boat suddenly start to slip backwards. The kayak stood vertically for a few milliseconds before it pirouetted backwards.

The world went silent. Ray looked up into a blue-green world, his capsized boat riding on the surface. As he waited for the crest of a wave to pass, he positioned his body and blade for a roll. With a short sweep of the paddle and a powerful downward stroke, he righted the boat and grabbed a breath of air just as a wave came crashing down on him, knocking the wind out of him, the powerful hydraulic force tossing the boat over.

Short of air, Ray went for a combat roll, fast and inelegant, breaking the surface just in time to paddle through the crest of the last large wave in the set. He gasped for air, his boat sideways, riding in the troughs. Then he started to search for Hanna.

He braced against the side of a wave. As his boat was carried to the crest, he could see the white hull of Hanna's kayak bobbing on the surface off his starboard side, the wind carrying her empty boat toward a distant shore. Then he caught sight of her, in deeper water, swimming with her paddle in the direction of her boat. He paddled after the kayak, eventually securing it with a short towline. Then he turned in Hanna's direction, fighting his way through another fierce set of waves, almost capsizing in the tempest.

As she clung to the deck lines of her kayak, he grabbed the strap of her PFD, pulled her across his deck, and then stuffed her in her cockpit. With his towline attached to her bow, he started paddling toward the lee of the headland and quiet water beyond. He knew that Hanna would be fighting to stay upright, her boat awash with water.

Once they were in protected waters, he slowed his pace, then briefly stopped. Hanna brought her boat next to his, and he unclipped the towline, and temporarily stuffed the rope under his PFD. They held the boats together for several minutes, breathing hard, each lost in their own thoughts.

Finally, Hanna said, "That was a little too much fun, and I need to empty my boat."

She paddled her boat toward shore, Ray following her. Once she reached the shallow water, Hanna rolled the kayak on its side and floated out. Grabbing the bow of the boat, she lifted it and waited as the water drained from the interior.

"Do you want to rest here for a few minutes or paddle to our launch point?" asked Ray.

"I'm getting cold. Let's go back now."

Twenty minutes later the boats were secured to the top rack, and Ray and Hanna sat in her Subaru, clad in fleece jumpsuits, looking out at the water, and drinking steaming coffee from a thermos.

"I'm sorry," she said.

"For what?"

She pointed toward the waves. "A hike or some quiet water would have been better. I talked you into this. It was crazy." She went silent for several minutes. "I was scared, Ray. I was out of control. I missed three or four rolls, something I never do. I had to come out of my boat. And when I tried to do a reentry roll, I lost control of my boat. And by that time I was starting to feel hypothermic."

Ray didn't immediately respond. "Look, we were only a few hundred yards off shore and the wind would have pushed us in that direction."

"Yes, but the wind and current together could have pushed us into the bay. We would have been a mile or two from shore. Again, I'm sorry." She gave him a clumsy embrace, leaning over the console and putting her arms around his neck. He pulled her tight and kissed her forehead. They clung together in silence.

17

Hanna slid from his arms as Ray reached for his phone. She watched his face as he listened.

"What's going on?" she asked as he switched off his phone.

"Missing child, three something, less than four, has wandered away from home. The mother doesn't know how long the little girl has been gone. She's a college student, taking online classes and lost track of the time. She assumed the child was playing outside with her older siblings. When they came in for dinner, she asked them to go back out and get their sister. They told her they hadn't seen her. They thought she was playing inside."

"What happens now?"

"Sue's started the process. We set up a command center, call in our people, and ask the township fire department for help." He gazed out of the window. "The light is starting to fade. I don't like this."

"Do you think the child could have been abducted?"

"I don't know," Ray answered. "Head toward 22, then north. It's about ten or twelve miles away."

As Hanna drove, Ray handled a flurry of calls, occasionally giving her further directions. The roads got smaller, finally ending up on a dusty gravel road that meandered through a rolling countryside, thick woods on each side encroaching on the narrow lane.

An array of police and fire vehicles were already parked in the sandy yard of the small frame house when they arrived. As he climbed out of the car, Ray surveyed the area. A battered pickup and an old, sagging Chevrolet were parked near the front porch.

The front door stood open. Ray entered. Sue stood near a sobbing woman held by a man who was trying to comfort her.

"What do we have?"

"Let's go outside," she said. Rain was beginning to fall. They stayed under the protection of the porch.

"The father was at work, the kids were playing outside. Mom was at the computer. Father comes home, and they discover the little girl is missing. The home has been thoroughly searched, Ray. That's the first thing I did, then the car and the pole building next. I've talked to the sister and brother—they're five and seven. They remember her playing with the dog. He's missing, too. Let me show you," she said, leading the way. The open area behind the house abutted a thick tangle of second growth pines and hardwoods. A thin, dark canopied path snaked through the woods.

"Where does it go?" asked Ray.

"Stays like this for about a quarter of a mile, then links up with a web of snowmobile and ATV paths. It's all federal or state forestland. The kids said she liked to play in there."

"How about the dog?"

"The father said the dog is her constant companion."

"That's probably a good thing, unless it decides to chase a deer or gets lured away by a pack of coyotes. How about time? How long has she been gone?"

"Hard to tell. Mother was totally hysterical when I got here. Father wasn't much help. He said when he got home they did a quick search, and then called 911. Based on what they told me, probably two to three hours, maybe more. A couple of volunteer firemen are bringing their ATVs." She paused a minute and looked at the sky. The daylight was starting to fade and the rain was intensifying. "I don't know how far a little girl could travel."

"Let's get the search organized," said Ray. "We need to cover a lot of territory, and hopefully we won't lose anyone in the process."

Sue took a call just as the group was clustering around a map she had laid out on the hood of her Jeep. "Good news, everyone," she announced. "Central has just had a call about a little girl found by a jogger. She's about three miles from here. We'll go pick her up. Please stay around until we can confirm that this is the right child."

With the child's mother in the passenger's seat, Sue led the way. Ray gave Hanna the details as she followed. They pulled into the circle drive of a contemporary lakefront home. A large door at the center swung open as they approached. A tall, thin female in a silver-gray running suit was framed by the warm interior lighting. The woman, who later identified herself as Joan Peacock, led the way to a spacious great room with a kitchen area off at one side.

"Mom, cocoa. Good cocoa," the small child squealed, showing no intention of leaving her booster seat at the kitchen table. A small, ragamuffin dog sat at the side of the toddler's chair, looking hopefully at the cookie she was waving in her hand.

The child's mother collapsed in tears as she hugged her daughter. A few minutes later, as the mother profusely thanked Peacock, Hanna checked Abigail over and gave Ray a reassuring nod.

"Run Abigail and her mother home," Ray said to Sue. "And once you're there, get all the information for the incident report. I'll get the details here, and we will put it together on Monday. And one more thing, thank everyone who came out to help. "

"How about social services?" Sue questioned.

"Let's talk about that on Monday."

As Sue was driving away, Mrs. Peacock observed, "You seem to be in charge."

Ray showed her his identification and apologized for not introducing himself earlier. "And this is Dr. Jeffers. We were kayaking. We had just gotten off the water when the call came in. I need to get some information from you. How did you happen to find the child?"

"I have this five mile route I follow. Part of it is through the woods. Lately I've been staying more to the road. It's getting dark earlier, and it's pretty remote. But today I just thought I was being silly, I mean I never see anyone in there. It was the dog that got my attention. I think he was standing guard. He started barking at me. The child, Abigail, was off the trail. Blueberries, she was looking for blueberries. She asked me if I would help her find blueberries. Her language is pretty good. I have grandchildren that age," she explained.

"I shouted, thinking there must be a parent around. Finally, I just picked her up, carried her home, and called 911. I was in a panic, but she seemed to be enjoying herself. She liked the attention, liked being held. And that little dog, he was at my heels the whole time watching out for her."

"You don't carry a cell?" There was concern in Ray's tone.

"Usually I do. I just had forgotten it."

Ray looked out through a wall of glass toward the lake, barely visible in the gloaming. "Beautiful home. You have a great view of the water."

"It's quite spectacular. When I sit here in the morning having coffee, I feel very privileged to live in such a beautiful spot."

"You live here alone?" asked Hanna.

"Yes," she answered, focusing on Hanna. "I think my story is a familiar one up here. My husband and I found this place years ago. There was an old log cottage on this spot that we enjoyed for a number of years. And as retirement approached we had that place torn down and we built our dream home. About a year after we moved here, he died. Heart attack. Not his first, but I thought once he got away from the pressures of his job, he'd be okay. After he passed, I didn't think I could continue to live here, but I've gotten used to it."

She looked at Ray and Hanna. "Are you a couple?"

A long silence followed. Finally, Hanna responded, "We're kayaking friends."

"You look good together. You look like you fit." A few moments later she asked, "Can I make you some coffee?"

"No, we should be going," said Ray. "My thanks to you. You may have saved a little girl's life."

She looked out the window into the encroaching darkness. "I guess there is a reason for me to be here."

They rode in silence as Hanna worked her way through the small roads back to the highway. Ray was thinking about all the tragic scenarios—everything from child molesters to wild animals—that had run through his consciousness before the little girl had been found.

"Are you okay?" Hanna asked.

"Better than okay. A happy ending."

"I was watching you. You became so quiet. Not that you weren't in command of the situation. Everyone looked to you for leadership. Maybe I'm over reading your reaction, but there seemed so much going on."

Ray thought about Hanna's comments. There was a lot going on.

"Did you ever think of having children, Ray?"

"It's been a topic a few times," he finally said. He was thinking about his long relationship with Ellen. They had talked about children over the years, but her long battle with cancer had ended those conversations. And then there was Ashleigh, the daughter he had never known, a memory still too painful for him to go back to.

"We've been hanging out together for a while, Elkins. I know nothing about you and you know almost nothing about me. I'm talking about our personal history, the backstory. Our relationship is always in the present."

"Is there a problem with that?" he asked.

Hanna was slow to respond. Finally she said, "No, I think it's a good thing. You've been a safe harbor. Thank you."

18

Hanna coarsely grated a chunk of Parmigiano Reggiano as Ray put the finishing touches on a pasta dish, a combination of oven-roasted parsnips, bacon, and heavy cream mixed with al dente farfalle. His concentration was on the food, the colors, textures, smells. At the end he tasted the mixture and adjusted the spices, judiciously adding a bit more salt and some coarsely ground black pepper. Then he spooned the mixture into a serving dish, carried it to the table, and lit some candles. The concerns of the day had been pushed into the background.

"Bon appétit," he said, lifting a wine glass.

"Looks and smells wonderful, Ray. Elegant comfort food, an absolutely perfect late evening dinner. Thank you." After several forkfuls, she said, "That Peacock woman, she thought we were a couple."

"Surprised she didn't think we were twins, same jumpsuits and same bright yellow storm cags."

"Yes, but we do wear our hair differently."

"There's that," said Ray.

"Are we a couple?"

Ray pointed to his mouth to signal he was still chewing. He was also buying time, thinking about a response. Hanna had arrived in his life just as another relationship was falling apart. In the beginning it was mostly about kayaking. In recent months they found they were spending most of their free time, on and off the water, together. "I don't know."

"I'm seeing you exclusively. By all appearances, the same is true with you."

"How could I see anyone else," laughed Ray. "I never know when you're going to come marching through the door, day or night."

"You don't seem to mind."

"No, I'm always happy to see you. In fact, when you don't arrive, especially when it's more than a day or two, I really miss your company."

"It's not that I want anything formal, Ray. I'm happy with the way things are. Is that okay?"

"Yes," said Ray, reaching over and putting his hand on hers.

"And this afternoon. I think I talked you into—"

"You didn't talk me into anything. I loved being out on the big lake, even if things got out of control. Eat while the food is still hot."

After the dishes were carried away, Hanna plated a small wedge of Stilton accompanied by crackers and thin slivers of apple. Ray filled two small glasses with port.

"You're looking at the last of the cheese," said Hanna. "The same for the Parmigiano. I think it's time for an emergency run to Zingerman's. Maybe we make a weekend of it. Take in a play or a concert. Ann Arbor is special to me, Ray. I'd like to be there with you.

"But not until you solve this murder. And this gives me a segue back to Mrs. Peacock's 'couple' remark. The reason this works, I'm talking about us, is because we accept certain things about one another. When you're in the middle of an investigation, you grow silent, your brain is engaged. You're totally preoccupied.

"I know I do a similar thing. I'm not through my PTSD, maybe never will be. You accept that about me. You don't make me feel like damaged goods when I'm struggling with things."

Ray was slow to respond. He was thinking about his own ghosts, but before he was able to verbalize his thoughts, she continued.

"There's something going on that I need to talk to you about." This time she reached across and took his hand. "I had a call from a friend at Stanford, someone I served with in the military who's now an associate dean in the medical school. They have an opening on a research team that would extend my skills. I'd earn a Ph.D. in the process. My future after that would probably be in research rather than clinical medicine."

Ray took a small sip of the tawny colored wine. He became apprehensive.

"It came out of the blue, Ray. It's not something I applied for. There's an old story in the medical community that when people go into the profession they think they can keep all their patients alive. When they find that they can't, some wander off and become researchers so they don't have to deal with that reality."

"Is that where you are?" asked Ray.

"I don't know. I'm highly conflicted. That's why I needed to be on the water today. I had to get my focus on something else. I wanted to tell you about it, but I didn't know how to do it. I know you are under a lot of pressure with this murder—"

"How long has this been going on?"

"Just a few days. I got a call Thursday evening when I was at the hospital, still business hours on the coast. In the recent past I've hoped for something like this. If he had called eight months ago, I would have been on the plane the next morning." She looked at Ray. "I told him I needed a few days to think about it. They'd like me to start on January 2."

Ray looked into her eyes. "I'd miss you greatly." He paused. "That said, I think we all have to follow our dreams. If you think that's your destiny, you should pursue it."

"Would you explore living somewhere else?"

"I don't think so. Not now. My life is here. The land, the water, the people, this is where I want to be. This is where I'm happy, where I think that I'm useful in some small way."

19

Ray awoke to the whirring of the coffee grinder, then the sound of the espresso machine. He moved around in the bed, stretching the sore muscles, first in his calves, then in his arms, back and neck. He sat on the edge of the bed for a few moments before he pushed himself to his feet.

"Ready for your cappuccino?" asked Hanna, ensconced in his heavy wool robe, the hem almost reaching the floor.

"Yes," he answered as he stretched again.

"Sore?" she asked.

"A bit. We shoveled a lot of water yesterday." He leaned against the kitchen island and watched her work at the espresso machine. There was grace and efficiency in her every movement. She turned and handed a coffee mug in his direction, then slid it past him. Setting it on the island, she slid her arms under his and pulled him into a tight embrace. He wrapped his arms around her. Neither of them said a word until Hanna broke the spell. "Drink your coffee. It's only good when it's hot. Just paraphrasing you," she said as she slipped from his arms.

"Looks like we've got company," Hanna said, looking toward the drive.

After Hanna unlocked the door, Sue rushed in, putting Simone, a Cairn terrier she and Ray co-parented in his arms. She turned her attention to Hanna. "I hoped you'd be here. Can you help me with something?"

Ray watched the two women talking in low voices, and then Hanna escorted Sue to the guest bedroom. He could tell by the tone of the conversation that he shouldn't intrude.

Several minutes later they emerged, Sue looking ashen.

"Do you want a cappuccino?" asked Hanna.

"No, I've got too much to do. When do you think you will know something?"

"I'll start making some calls tomorrow morning. Hopefully, I can get things started before the end of the workday."

Sue collected Simone from Ray's arms. "It would probably be easier if I left her with you, but I need the company."

"Would you like breakfast?"

"No, I've got too much to do. But I'd like to go over things with you early in the day tomorrow."

"I will be in the office before 8:00."

"What's going on?" asked Ray, after Sue's departure.

"Sue found a lump in her right breast when she was showering this morning. There's a long history of breast cancer on her mother's side of the family. She's extremely frightened. I palpated both breasts. I could easily feel the mass that she is worried about. I'm surprised she didn't find it earlier. It's not insignificant."

"So what happens now?"

"She wants to go to Mayo. That's where her mother was successfully treated. And I agreed with her, I think it's a good choice."

"Wouldn't it be more convenient to be seen locally, at least initially?"

"Yes. That said, things really move fast at the big clinics. You can have four or five appointments in a day or two. Sue will quickly have a diagnosis and a choice of treatment plans. It's the uncertainty, Ray, that's what's hard to deal with. Ray, you know this woman well. From everything you've said, she's usually a rock. But you just saw her. She's falling apart. I would bet she's more frightened now than ever before in her life. And it's more than dying, something we all fear. It's all about a woman's body image, her sexuality, her perceived desirability. And for a young woman like Sue, it's also about finding a mate, childbearing, nursing. We have these multiple selves. Yes, we now have professional lives of our own, but there are the primordial urges, also. It's all so complex. I'm doing a lousy job trying to articulate what's going on."

"I understand," said Ray. "When you asked about children....I was thinking about my long-term companion, Ellen. She died of breast cancer. Even now I can't talk about the sadness, horror, and loss. And a few years later I became my mother's caregiver during her final months. Breast cancer, again."

Hanna moved into his arms.

"Sue, she's so young. This shouldn't happen," said Ray.

"With a little luck, this will be eminently treatable. It's too early to start worrying."

20

Ray's focus was fixed on answering an email when Simone landed in his lap, demanding his full attention. Several minutes later Sue appeared, carrying her laptop under one arm and a stack of documents under the other.

"How are you today?" asked Ray.

"My house is clean. I'm packed and ready to go whenever things are in place. And I'm less frantic than yesterday."

After arranging things on the conference table, she continued, "I had planned to spend time yesterday going through Gillian's devices. It didn't happen. I won't tell you I didn't think about Gillian's death, it's always sort of there. It's just that my own stuff got in the way. Emma, one of my yoga friends, called. I told her about, well, you know. I don't know if she phoned or texted people, but the other women friends started calling. Then Emma rang me back, said they were going to have a healing circle at her studio. She does fiber art, has a big open space in her studio. Simone was invited, too. So we all showed up in the late afternoon in our yoga clothes, and Emma lead us through our usual practice. Then we formed a circle and held hands. Simone sat in the center. She looked totally confused by what was going on.

"People shared stories of healing, intimate things that I was unaware of for the most part. I don't know how to explain it, Ray. My former cynical self, if I were looking in from the outside, would have called this really hokey. It wasn't. I felt cared for and protected. I had a sense of calm, at least for a while. Afterwards, there were all kinds of wine and food—vegetarian.

"Simone and I crashed when we got home. But somewhere during the night I had this nightmare. I could see every detail of the vineyard, not like we saw it in daylight. I was viewing it by moonlight. It was monochromatic, blacks, greys, and silvers with a hint of blue. I could feel the warmth of someone close behind me, then the arm encircling my neck. Then I knew I was about to die. And…"

"What?" asked Ray.

"Just as I was about slip away, Simone started licking my face, and I woke up. Then she wrapped herself around my head. I guess she decided I needed protection. So, for awhile I was wide awake, thinking about the case."

"Me too," said Ray. "From 3:00 to sometime before my alarm went off. I'd like to see the photos again. The ones Gillian took at the wineries. My memory is that you had only time to look through the photos from eight wineries. I'd like to quickly go through the rest. Could you put them up as thumbnails. I want to be able to scan the whole collection and see if she ever deviated from her usual pattern."

"Give me a few, Ray. Let me figure out how to do that. Maybe you can get us some fresh coffee."

When Ray returned with a carafe of hot coffee, the large, high definition screen on the wall was covered with dozens of photos.

"Is this what you are looking for?"

"Yes," he answered.

"They are organized by time, in the order they were taken."

"Perfect. Now would you slowly scroll through them?"

Ray stood at her side watching the rows of photos move up the screen and then disappear.

"Did you see what I've just seen?" Sue asked.

"Yes," said Ray. "That series doesn't fit the pattern. Start at the beginning and make them full size."

The sign from the Terroir Nord Winery filled the screen.

"Who is that?" asked Sue. "What did he do to deserve…let me see…16 snapshots when everyone else got one or two at best?"

They could see the young man was talking as he poured wine. There were several photos with the man holding the bottle so Gillian could get a good picture of the label.

"Looks like there was some flirting going on, at least on his part. Too bad she wasn't shooting some selfies at the same time. I'd like to see how she was playing it. Who's the guy? He's very cute. Looks like he's about my age, too."

"Marty Donaldson has a couple of boys, twins I think. That's probably one of them. Marty mentioned that a daughter-in-law works in the tasting room, so at least one of the boys is married. When were these taken?"

"Wednesday morning, early. Ray, I'm sorry I didn't survey all the photos before. I got too busy building my chronology."

"We need to talk to this person," said Ray, "and find out why he got all the special attention." He moved to the large whiteboard and added *Interview Donaldsons' sons* to the task list.

"Sue, go through the rest of Terroir Nord photos slowly. And make them full size now."

"Oh, my God," said Sue as a picture of the vineyard where Gillian Mouton's body was found filled the screen.

"Go through the rest," said Ray.

After he viewed them all, he said, "She was there. Was this part of a special tour or did she run down there on her own. Would you print me copies of the tasting room photos and the ones from the vineyard. Having a chat with the brothers is the first order of business."

As the printer whirred behind Ray's desk, Sue retrieved some papers from a folder, passing one to Ray and holding on to the second one. "I did manage to make a list of Gillian's recent phone calls Saturday morning before I left the office. As you can see, Gillian wasn't a Chatty Cathy. Very few calls, most of short duration, and I would guess they all are directly connected to her business. I've made notes about the callers and recipients."

"The series of calls to a 312—?"

"It's a cell number. The woman is from Chicago, lives here now. Her name is Blythe Erickson. I talked with her before I left the office Saturday. She was going to be involved with Gillian's tasting event. The woman is a chef and cheese maker, and she was supposed to do the pairings for the event. They had a planning meeting last Monday. We need to sit down with her." She looked across at Ray and smiled. "Artisanal goat cheese, Ray, chévre. Saw an article about her in *Traverse Magazine*. Pretty woman. You'd be the perfect person to interview her."

21

It was nearing 9:00 by the time Ray arrived at the Terroir Nord Winery. The foliage on the lofty maples that lined the narrow drive to the winery created a crimson arbor. The small gravel parking area near the modest tasting room was already crowded with vehicles, most with downstate or out-of-state plates. Ray, in mufti, entered the building and blended in with the crowd. He watched a younger version of Marty Donaldson, lean and blond, the man Ray had seen in Gillian's photos, working a flock at the tasting counter. His audience was composed of people mostly in their 60s and 70s, retirees up to see the color and tour the wineries.

"All our private label wines are made with estate-grown grapes. Our vineyards are free of pesticides and herbicides. Our grapes are harvested at the moment they reach full maturity. Within hours of harvesting, grapes are crushed and the process of creating a great artisanal wine is underway."

Donaldson had a standard patter about each wine that he delivered as he moved down the row making one ounce pours into waiting glasses. After the pour he carefully moved his spectators through the steps of wine sampling, telling them what to look for as they sniffed, tasted, swallowed, and waited for the aftertaste. At the end, the crowd was skillfully moved to a twenty-something woman who answered questions and handled the sales.

As Donaldson cleared away the glasses in preparation for the next group, Ray moved in quickly. Donaldson glanced down at Ray's ID as he started to wipe off the bar.

"You're one of Marty's sons, right?"

"Yes, I'm Randy," he answered, his welcoming smile disappearing. "We need to talk."

"Is it something that can wait, Sheriff? As you can see, I have people standing in line."

"It will only take a few minutes. I'd like you to tell me about this." Ray opened a folder with the collection of 8" by 10" copies of the photos of Donaldson standing behind the bar.

Randy caught the attention of the woman in the sales area. "I'll be back in a few," he said before leading Ray out a side door.

"What's this all about?" he demanded. "It's bad enough that... what did she call herself...the Wine Bitch got killed on our property. Now we're being harassed when we're busy as hell."

Ray slowly inhaled, then locked eye-to-eye with Randy Donaldson. He opened the folder again. "I have a few questions. I expect your cooperation."

"Go ahead. Let's get this over with. But you're wasting your time. I know nothing about the woman or her death."

"There are twenty odd photos of you here, Randy. We've looked at hundreds of Gillian Mouton's photos. She only collected a few photos at the other wineries she visited. How is it that she seemed to take such a special interest in you?"

Randy looked away, biting his lower lip, then back at Ray. "She was probably just killing time. Anyway, you can shoot that many pics in 15 or 20 seconds."

"True," said Ray. "But these are all date and time stamped. They were taken the morning she was killed. And they were taken over the course of an hour, not 20 seconds. Did you know Gillian Mouton?"

"Sheriff, everyone in the business knew her. You can hardly open a wine magazine without seeing an article about her or one of her ads."

"I didn't ask about her notoriety, I asked if you knew her. It looks like the two of you had an extended conversation."

"Well, if you look at the time stamps, you will see that she was here early, an hour before we opened. I was organizing and restocking for the day. She knocked on the window. I opened the door to tell her we were closed, to come back later. But she weaseled her way in."

"Did you recognize her?"

"I didn't have to. She immediately made clear who she was, and that I should give her my undivided attention. So I did. What the hell, lots of sales follow her recommendations. I did a full tasting, including some of the wines that are still in development."

"You'd met her before?"

"I'd seen her at trade shows. She was good at working the crowds."

"You're telling me you knew her by reputation and sight, nothing more?"

"Like I said, I've seen her. Sometimes she was working her booth. Other times she was giving a talk or participating on a panel."

"But never one to one, like having a conversation over a glass of wine, something like that."

"Correct," said Randy, beginning to look more relaxed with the direction of the conversation.

Ray fanned all the pictures. "How did you rate this special attention?"

"Mouton, she was very positive about the wine I was giving her to be sampled. She did some longer stories on her website under a heading of *Wineries to Watch*. She mentioned that she might like to write about our operation. Sheriff, I was doing my best to please the woman. Do you know what that kind of publicity would mean for us?"

"Tell me."

"Sales, store placement. Restaurant placement. It would put us on the map. Now it's not going to happen. The only publicity we've gotten is negative."

Ray slowly removed three photos from the back of the stack. As he handed them to Randy, he asked, "Can you tell me about these?"

Randy looked at a photo showing an open gate and a vineyard stretching vertically beyond. Slowly, he moved to the next photo, obviously taken just inside the gate, showing the terraced hillside covered with trellises. Finally, he looked at the last picture, a close-up of a cluster of black-blue Cabernet Franc grapes. He looked at them a second time, slowly, then handed them back to Ray.

"Well?" asked Ray.

"What do you want from me, Sheriff?"

"Those were taken shortly after the last of the interior shots with you. As you know, we found her body at that location the next morning. Do you want to tell me about this?"

"Nothing to tell, really. I gave her a taste of one of our new reds, something we haven't sold yet. The first batch is still in barrels. She liked it, wanted to know what we were blending. I told her we had Merlot and Cabernet Franc on the same hillside. We were blending grapes from the same terroir to make a very special wine. She said she wanted to see it, wanted a couple of pictures for the article, so I took her down there. It's just a few minutes down the road."

"Did you drive her?"

"No. I took a truck, and she followed. She was running late to wherever she was going next. She wanted to leave from there."

Ray moved in close. "Mouton ends up getting killed there sometime during the night and neither you nor your father mention that she was here or that you and she took this little side trip?"

"My father didn't know. It was just me."

"Why didn't you contact us? This is a murder investigation."

"I didn't see how it had anything to do with anything. I didn't want to get involved."

"Was she still in the vineyard when you left?"

"No, she had me parked in. She left before me."

"Did you arrange to meet her there later in the evening?"

"No way, Sheriff. Not a chance."

"Did you ever see her again?"

"No."

"How about email, texts, phone calls."

"No. Why would I?"

"Where were you Wednesday night, Thursday in the early a.m.?"

"Wednesday…I was here till late running the crusher."

"What time was that?"

"Probably close to ten."

"Anyone here with you?" asked Ray

"Shane, he's a high school kid. He was cleaning up when I left."

"Then what did you do?"

"I went home and showered and went to bed. It had been a twelve-hour workday."

"Where's home?"

"Just down the road, the old Bazinski farm. I'm redoing the farmhouse."

"Anyone see you?"

"No. I live alone."

"So you were what, a mile or two from the murder scene?"

"Less than a mile."

"And you had been at the murder scene with the victim earlier in the day."

"Pure happenstance. I had no reason to kill her. She could have done us a world of good. Sheriff, I have to get back to work. I have nothing more to say unless I have a lawyer at my side."

22

Ray turned off the highway onto a small gravel road and followed the signs to the Chévre Craft Farm. The drive to the business ended in a small parking lot just beyond an old barn. A worn Volvo station wagon, its blue exterior dull and faded, was parked near a stone pathway leading to the interior.

Ray walked into the sales area, a small room constructed in a front corner of the barn. He studied the cheeses in the display unit, then pushed the plunger on a call bell a couple of times and waited. When there was no response, he walked through a door at the back of the room and followed the sound of machinery to the interior of the creamery. He found a woman rinsing down stainless steel counters and assorted equipment with a stream of steaming water. She jumped when she finally saw him and switched off the pressure washer.

"Sheriff Elkins?"

"Yes," he answered, showing her his identification.

"Blythe Erickson," she said, drying her right hand on her lab coat before extending it in Ray's direction. "Sorry, I didn't hear you. I was just trying to get the final washing up done. Let's sit outside. Would you like some tea?"

Ray answered to the affirmative and watched as she hung her lab coat and a hairnet on a peg near the door and traded her dark-green rubber wellies for a pair of well-used Birkenstocks. A few minutes later they were sipping tea at a picnic table at the side of the barn. Ray guessed Blythe to be in her middle forties. A small woman, she moved with the grace of a dancer. Her long blond hair was pulled into a tight bun.

"On the phone you said you needed to talk about Gillian Mouton. I was devastated by the news of her death, Sheriff. She was an amazing person."

"Ms. Erickson—"

"Blythe, please, Sheriff."

"Your name was on her calendar, and we noted also that she had called you and that you were doing the food pairings for her wine event. We're just in the beginning of this investigation. We know so little about Ms. Mouton. I was hoping you might be able to provide some background information. Maybe there was something in your conversations or something you observed that might help us with our inquiries."

"Sheriff, Gillian—what an interesting woman. Sadly, I can't say I really knew her. We only spent a limited amount of time together."

"How did you meet?" asked Ray.

"At a food and wine show in New York."

"When was that?"

"February, toward March, a good time to be out of here for a week or two. I was staying with a college friend who lives in Westchester. And I went to the show as a way of getting information and to also do some networking. I'm still trying to understand this business. Gillian had a booth. I'm sure by now you know all about her newsletter and blog."

"Yes."

"She was one of the keynotes, did a fantastic job. Later I dropped by her booth. The badges, our IDs, had our names with the city and state below. As soon as she noticed where I was living, she got all excited. Told me about her connections to this area. And she asked me to accompany her to a special dinner that evening being put on by one of the major wine distributors."

Blythe looked away as she thought back to that evening, then back at Ray. "It was an exquisite evening in an amazing venue, the Kunsthalle in the MoMA. She introduced me to top chefs in the country. Most of the people I had only seen on television. There were lots of the most celebrated personalities in the wine industry, and Gillian knew all of them. She was totally at ease. And the food, I probably made a spectacle taking pictures with my iPhone. The presentations were fabulous. And the wine, expensive and exclusive, flowed freely. I imagine I looked like a bit of a provincial, I wasn't dressed for that kind of event. And Gillian, she just knew everyone. She was a people magnet.

"Things went very late, and I was worried about getting back to Westchester. She sensed my discomfort and suggested I spend the night with her. I texted my friend so she wouldn't be worried and stayed with Gillian. Do you know New York?" she asked.

"Not well, just enough to get to museums, Lincoln Center, and the airports."

"Well, Gillian had this great apartment in West Village. It was an old brick apartment building, three or four floors as I remember. It was a beautiful space, 50s modern furniture—high quality reproductions, not the original stuff. Her kitchen was tiny, but incredibly well done.

She was the perfect hostess. She went out of her way to make sure I was comfortable. And the next morning, earlier than I perhaps would have liked, she took me to this fantastic bakery for coffee and chocolate croissants. The neighborhood was totally cool.

"And while I was luxuriating over cappuccino and pastry, Gillian was on task. She wanted to know where I was trained as a chef, how many years I lived in Paris and Provence, and about my training as a cheese maker. And then she shifted to this area. She had a whole series of questions about the wineries and the personalities connected to them. At the time I didn't think much about it, but since her death…well, I don't know how to articulate what I'm thinking."

"Did you spend any more time with her while you were in New York?"

"I did. We went back to the convention center, and she actually asked me to help with her booth, handing out brochures, that sort of thing. She had a couple of women she'd hired for the event to handle sales of her newsletter. I enjoyed watching her. She was flamboyant, energetic, and very funny.

"She took me to dinner that evening as a thank you for helping at her booth. And over dessert and coffee she asked me if I would be interested in providing the food for her Michigan event in the fall. Obviously, for me this was an incredible outcome. And since that time we were in regular contact over the arrangements."

"When was the last time you saw Gillian?"

"Only once after New York. And that was a week ago Monday. She came by to look over the final menu. She suggested a few changes and sampled some of the cheeses I had prepared for special pairings. By the time she left, everything was pretty much in place."

"Did she share anything about other people she was meeting here?"

"No. We only did business. She was totally focused on the event." Blythe stopped for a minute. "There was one thing, nothing personal, but she asked if I had heard that Ursidae Winery was moving into the export business. I told her I'm really out of the loop on industry gossip. I'm working night and day to try to get this business off the ground."

"Did she mention any relationships, men she might be seeing in the area?"

"Nothing like that. She didn't give much away about her personal life." Blythe paused. "Is there anything else?"

"When she mentioned Ursidae, did she mention Phillip Lovell specifically?"

"Sometime along the way in one of our early conversations, she said they had the best event space, and Lovell would make sure everything went perfectly."

"How about Randy Donaldson? Did Gillian mention him?"

"She introduced me in New York. He was hanging around the booth, almost being a nuisance. Later that evening she told me she had had a one-night stand at some event. He'd been a pain ever since."

"Did she talk about relationships, people she might be involved with?"

"Not really. We didn't spend any time on that. She did say something to the effect that she was too busy to clutter her life with a serious relationship."

"How did you find her, Gillian?" asked Ray. "Did you like her?"

Blythe was slow to answer. Ray noted how her hazel eyes blended with her bronze skin and blond hair. Her face was free of makeup save a small hint of lip gloss. She had the kind of natural look he found very attractive.

"I admired her and what she'd accomplished in just a few short years. She made a name for herself in a rather stodgy, mostly male-dominated business. She was very skilled at teaching about wine, especially to her target audience of young, professional women.

"That said, Gillian and I were very different. She was on the marketing end. And I got the impression her business required lots of cash. She had to be out there hustling all the time. I'm trying to do something very different, a farm with a small herd of goats that will generate enough of a cash flow to provide me with a modest living. I want to have the time to enjoy this," she made a sweeping motion with her hand.

"Before you go, I want you to try this chévre. It's more in the French style, a bit smelly with some lovely mold. Not anything that I would try to sell here, yet. Perhaps in a few years. Your reputation as a foodie precedes you, so while I have you here…."

Ray pushed the cheese knife through the crust into the runny cheese. He carefully spread it on a thin slice of baguette.

"How is it?" she asked as he slowly chewed.

"Exquisite," he answered as he savored the distinctive flavor.

23

Ray watched the weary, early morning travelers advancing toward security, most dragging carry-on bags. He shared their fatigue. There were no smiles or cheerful greetings, just a purposeful column, like a defeated army in retreat, lining up to be benignly badgered before being herded onto a small, crowded aircraft.

Hanna came to his side, arm against arm. In the distance he could see Sue Lawrence, talking with a counter attendant. The terminal smelled of coffee, with an occasional hint of cigarette smoke carried in from the outside.

"I'm surprised she wants me to make this trip with her," said Hanna, looking in Sue's direction.

"Why wouldn't she? You're a doctor, you know that medical center, and you did all the legwork to get her seen immediately."

"All true, but there are things you don't seem to understand, Ray." She slid her arm through his.

"What am I missing?"

Hanna, her eyes still glued on Sue, moved closer. "Sue is in love with you, Ray. She tolerates me. Right now she's frightened, and she needs a friend, a doctor friend."

Ray started to protest, Hanna cut him off. "We're not talking about logic, Ray, it's about feeling."

He absorbed her last comment. Finally, he asked, "Do you have a timeline?"

"If we get out of here on schedule and make the connecting flight in Minneapolis, Sue's first appointment is at ten, Central

Time. I don't know how things will unfold after that. A biopsy, the pathology, it can all happen today. If surgery is required, then tomorrow or the next day. I've cleared my schedule for the next two days, but I can stay the rest of the week, if that's necessary. I'll email you as things unfold."

"Let's go," Sue's remark was directed at Hanna. She then gave Ray a quick hug. "Take care." Then she marched toward security towing her carry-on. Hanna and Ray followed, embracing a last time, then separating as Hanna moved to join the line.

Ray stood for a long moment and watched the two women start to pile their possessions in the ubiquitous gray plastic bins, and then turned and headed for his car. Simone, the terrier, was curled up in the driver's seat. He gently herded her to the passenger side and climbed in.

The first glimmers of dawn were creeping over the horizon as he drove north along the bay. Ray was lost in thought. Hanna had not delivered any new information, but Ray had always done his best to avoid thinking about his feelings toward Sue. She was such an important part of his daily life, a colleague, a companion, and a friend, but never a lover. And since they started co-parenting Simone the previous winter, in some ways they functioned even more like a couple.

On one occasion, after too much champagne, they almost crossed the line. Ray pulled back at the last minute. Close to a year had passed since then.

From early on in her employment with the department and the ensuing development of their friendship, he kept reminding himself that he was her boss and any romantic link, even a casual encounter, would probably bring more sorrow than joy and possibly end their professional relationship. Ray's admiration for Sue remained, but since Hanna Jeffers had come into his life, Ray was better able to keep his feelings for Sue in perspective.

"Unit seven, are you in service?" Ray's introspection was interrupted by the sound of the police radio.

"Go ahead, central."

"What's your 20?"

"Nearing the center of sector 2."

"Switch to phone."

Ray pulled to the side of the road and waited for the call. "What's going on?" he asked.

"We have a report of an explosion and fire at the Cedar Bay Marina. Fire and rescue have been dispatched. Fire has requested additional assets."

"Injuries or deaths?"

"No information at present."

"I'll be on the scene in a few minutes," said Ray.

Being unfamiliar with Sue's Jeep, it took him a few seconds to find the toggle switches for the light bar and siren. He could see the thick black smoke long before he reached Cedar Bay. Two blocks into the four-block-long business district, he made a right turn and traveled less than a hundred yards to the parking area overlooking the marina. Ray worked with two of his young deputies, Brett Carty and Barbara Sinclair, to maintain a safety perimeter to keep the increasing crowd of gawkers away from the area.

Below he could see the village fire engine idling near the end of the dock, the sound of its big diesel engine almost lost in the roar of the blaze. Fire personnel scurried to get equipment deployed. The suction hose used to pull water from the lake to the pumper was already in place. Then attack hoses were attached, the diesel labored as the pump was engaged, and the firefighters directed the powerful jets of water at the remains of a boat and surrounding dock area that was also engulfed in flames. Soon the inferno, a roaring red-orange tongue at the base of a billowing pillar of sooty smoke, was brought under control and extinguished. In the process, the boat, already burned to the waterline, disappeared below the surface of the water.

Ray found the fire captain, Bernie Rathman, as Rathman's crew worked to extinguish the last few hotspots in the old wooden pier.

"What happened?"

"Hard to say," replied Rathman. "The boat was mostly gone when we got here. Dispatch said something about an explosion.

When we got here the boat and dock were fully engaged. Flames on the water, too. Must have had a lot of gas onboard."

"Any casualties?"

"I suspect so. But I didn't see anyone. Explosion like that's probably not survivable. Most likely a case of gas fumes in the bilge and some kind of spark. Can we get your dive team to go down there?"

"Yes, I'll get that organized."

"And a crane, too. Need to get what's left out of the water and contain what's left of the oil and gas that was onboard."

Sometime after noon Ray stood near Dr. Dyskin as he knelt near the body that had just been carried from the water by members of the dive team. Dyskin methodically examined the body from head to foot, muttering to himself as he went. With the help of an EMT, he rolled the body over and continued his inspection of the remains. He paused for a moment and worked at removing a wallet, then turned and held it out in Ray's direction.

Ray grasped the cold, wet leather for several seconds, then slowly opened it and looked at the drivers' license. His suspicions were confirmed. Gregory Mouton peered up at him from the small photo in the lower left side of the document. *Gillian, now Gregory, what the hell's going on here?*

Ray moved closer to the body, the lower extremities already in a body bag. "I need a good look at the victim."

Dyskin moved to the side, giving him a clear view of the man's visage. The man's face was badly damaged by blunt force trauma, but it was clearly Gregory Mouton.

Dyskin, now standing at his side said, "I'll know more after the autopsy. My guess would be that he died instantly from massive internal trauma. The explosion was from behind the victim's back, propelling him against the steering wheel and whatever else was up there. The chest was crushed inward, ribs broken. There are probably massive brain injuries as well."

He paused briefly, "You okay?"

Ray held the open wallet in Dyskin's direction. "The woman in the vineyard, this is her stepbrother."

"So is this a suspicious death or a cruel coincidence?" asked Dyskin.

A line from Macbeth flashed across Ray's consciousness. *And the right-valiant Banquo walk'd too late....*

"A suspicious death until it's proven otherwise," said Ray.

24

Ray peered through the screen door on the front porch into the shadows of the interior of the house before he pushed the doorbell. He heard a chime sound deep within. Then Sherry Mouton appeared, saying, "I'm sorry, Sheriff, Gregory isn't here. He's down at the boat getting it ready to...." Then the greeting smile disappeared. Ray could see a wave of uncertainty cross her countenance. "What's happened, Sheriff?"

"May I come in?"

"Please."

They settled into chairs at the vintage kitchen table. Ray looked carefully at Sherry for the first time.

"There was an explosion and fire at the marina," Ray explained.

"Was Gregory injured?"

It took a few seconds for Ray to respond. He sensed she knew the answer before he started speaking. "Your husband didn't survive the explosion. We've recovered his body."

Ray sat quietly as she collapsed in tears. After several minutes, he asked, "Is there someone I can call, someone who can stay with you?"

"I need to get some tissue," she said, heading toward an adjacent room.

When she returned, she said, "I've always been afraid of that boat." She started sobbing again, then slowly regained control. "It was damaged by an explosion before, sometime early in our marriage. Gregory and his father hauled it up to the old barn," she motioned toward a building at the back of the property. "It sat in there for years, almost disappearing under the junk that got tossed on it. Old Mike was a real pack rat. Greg wasn't much better.

"When Mike started going downhill, Gregory hauled it out and started on a restoration. He said his dad needed something to live for. *Happy Daze*, that's the name they painted on the back. I have to admit, working together on that boat, it was good for both of them. Sadly, old Mike passed before the *Happy Daze* ever saw water again."

She looked off into the distance, chewing on a lip, and then wiping away tears. "Tell me what happened."

"I don't know for sure. There were a number of 911 calls reporting an explosion. When the fire crew arrived, the boat was almost completely destroyed. It sank as they were putting out the fire. The body was recovered by one of our divers."

A long silence followed. Finally she asked, "How did he...?"

"The medical examiner believes your husband was killed instantly by the force of the explosion."

Another long silence. "This was the day he was taking it over to the boatyard to be put in dry dock for the winter. All he was doing was moving the boat a few hundred yards."

"You said the *Happy Daze* had been damaged before?"

"Yes, a family story that was retold so many times, usually with much laughter. Like I said, it happened years ago."

"So what's the story?"

"We were downstate when it happened. We heard about it after. As I remember, it was something about Mike, that's Gregory's father, starting the boat one morning and the engine blowing up. His dog jumped into the water after the explosion, and Mike followed, thinking he needed to save the dog. In the end, Mike held on to the dog's collar, and the dog paddled to shore. So the dog did the rescuing. That was the joke, Mike was saved by his Portuguese water dog."

She paused briefly. "When they first pulled the Chris Craft out of the barn and got all the rubbish out of it, the boat didn't look too bad on the outside. The damage was in the back of the boat. There were supposed to be doors covering the engine. They were missing. Mike said they just found bits and pieces of the doors after the explosion.

"When Greg started on this restoration thing, I kept saying 'How are you going to keep it from blowing up a second time?' He told me the technology was much better now. They were adding all the improvements that modern boats have, things like blowers or fans, to make sure it could never happen again." She paused briefly. "I just wanted him to get rid of it. 'It's a collector's boat,' he said, 'worth a lot of money these days.' I kept saying we needed cash more than some damn boat. I think I had almost convinced him to part with it. Now this."

Ray let her comment hang for several seconds. "I've contacted the Fire Investigations Unit of the Michigan State Police. One of their officers will examine what's left of the boat. We will do our best to find the cause of the explosion and fire. But it's not always possible to make a definite determination."

Ray waited for a minute before saying, "Gillian was murdered. Now Gregory is dead. Is there anything you think I should know?"

Sherry stared off at the world beyond the glass doors, toward the bay and the peninsula beyond. "That was running through my mind, Sheriff, as soon as you told me."

"Did your husband share with you any concerns about his own safety?"

"No. Not that any of us ever know our partners completely, but I don't think so."

"The family business, any residual problems after it closed? Any creditors out there still…."

"Nothing like that, Sheriff. Our creditors didn't get 100 percent when our friendly banker cut off our short-term credit line and the business finally collapsed, but no one got hurt too badly. Other than us, of course. Sheriff, we live quietly here. We have no enemies."

"Gillian didn't mention being in any trouble when she talked with you and Gregory?"

"No, she didn't tell him anything."

She briefly collapsed in tears, then said, "Gregory's body, Sheriff."

"Because of the nature of his death, I've requested a forensic autopsy. The body has been sent to Grand Rapids. It should be available in a few days."

Ray passed her his card. "If something comes to mind, or if you need help with anything, please call." He paused briefly, "Do you have family or a friend close by that you can call? It would be good if you had someone with you."

"My neighbors, the next house over, they've become like family."

"Why don't you call them," said Ray. "I'll wait till they get here or walk over with you."

25

When Ray arrived back at the marina, the crane from the local boatyard had been moved to the scene, and the remains of the *Happy Daze* were being lifted from the water in a sling of thick nylon webbing secured under the hull. Once the boat was completely out of the water, the crane operator allowed the water to drain from the wreckage before slowly pivoting a hundred and eighty degrees. The operator leaned out of a window and yelled something to another worker on the ground who was helping guide the boat with a rope attached to one of the slings. The hull was then gently lowered, the blackened remains coming to rest on a grassy park near the entrance to the marina. Then the rattle of the diesel engine died away.

When he reached the boat, Brett Carty, the head of the sheriff department's marine unit, still clad in a wetsuit, was looking over the wreckage. Rory Tate, another of the younger deputies, was at his side.

"The next step," said Ray, "is to see if we can find any witnesses. Ask dispatch for the names and addresses of all the 911 callers. Talk to each of them. Then canvass the area. We're looking for anyone who might have seen the explosion or anything suspicious in the hours before, including last night. Other than this boat, the marina is empty, so any late night or early morning traffic might have caught someone's attention."

"What's going on?" asked Rory.

"The victim is Gregory Mouton," Ray explained. He's the stepbrother of…."

"Gillian," said Carty. "I can see why you want to give this a close look."

As Ray watched his young deputies march off, Mike Ogden, an arson investigator with the state police, backed his blue Suburban down the hill, stopping near the burned-out shell.

"Hey, Ray," Ogden called as he opened the rear doors of the vehicle. After retrieving a camera, he came to Ray's side.

Ray explained the murder of Gillian Mouton, now followed by the death of her stepbrother.

"I understand your suspicions. I'll give it my best shot, but as you can see there's nothing much here. Any witnesses?"

"We're working on that now," said Ray.

Ogden circled the boat, carefully photographing the remains from every angle. "Like I said, not much left—bit of the keel, these two main stringers, lower portion of some ribs, and some planking. Then there's that little flathead six. Hard to destroy a cast-iron block, but all of the ancillaries are gone. I'm surprised the mounting bolts held the engine to the stringers."

"Is there enough to establish a probable cause?"

"We can rule things out. I can take some samples and test for explosive materials other than gasoline, if you're wondering if there was some kind of bomb. Frankly, I don't think we'll find anything. This explosion appears to have been fueled by gasoline fumes. Whether it was caused by some kind of equipment failure or human meddling is another question. And the meddling part would be extremely hard to prove with what's left here. Now if you had a witness or two who can testify that they saw someone carrying a container of some kind in this direction…or messing around in the engine compartment…."

"Walk me through a fuel explosion, the accidental kind, then explain how someone could fiddle with things to make one happen."

"I start with a caveat," said Ogden. "I don't work on these very often. Marine explosions and fires are more common near metro Detroit where you have a high concentration of pleasure craft. You know, around Lake St. Clair and Port Huron. Most happen during or just after a boat has been fueled. My memory is that they are usually attributed to leaking or missing seals around the engine compartments or problems with fuel pumps and gas lines. As soon as the operator starts the engine, an errant spark from somewhere in the electric system ignites the fumes. And then you have a tragedy that looks like this one."

"The victim's wife told me that the rear area of the boat had been damaged before by some kind of explosion years ago. When her husband began restoring the boat, he told her it couldn't happen again because he was adding blowers and fans and all the modern stuff."

"But did he?" said Ogden. "Lots of guys say lots of things to appease wives and girlfriends. If he was trying to keep the boat original, he might have skipped that step, or it might have turned out to be more work than he wanted to do."

Ogden looked back at the boat and slowly circled it again. "Look Ray, when it comes to the construction and mechanics of wooden boats, I'm out of my league. And boat fires, maybe one percent of my investigations. But I can tell you a few things about gasoline, engines, and things that cause explosions. The first thing, gasoline is extremely explosive." Ogden pointed at his truck. "If I put thirty gallons in that beast, the controlled explosions in the engine will push the 3-ton vehicle what, 400 or 500 hundred miles. Now think about this boat. You never saw it before, right?"

"Correct."

"But you've seen antique runabouts like this, Ray. Try to visualize what used to be here. If this was a runabout design, there was a huge engine compartment at the rear. The top of it was covered with carefully fitted planking. In the middle was a cockpit area with a couple of bench seats. And at the front, another beautifully decked area. Here in the stern were hatches that provide access to the engine." Ogden moved closer to the skeleton, using his hands to show positions. "At both ends of this decked area, there were highly polished surface vents, probably made of brass and chrome plated. Some facing forward, some back, probably two and two. Engines need to breathe. When you're bouncing along on the waves, there would be a lot of natural ventilation. Sitting still at a dock, not so much.

"So what do you need for an explosion? Fumes and a spark. Let's say there was a modest fuel leak, like where that copper fuel line, or what's left of it, runs into the carburetor. Lots of heat and vibrations in that environment—things shake loose, metal fatigues. And let's say the spark plug wires have deteriorated and are shorting against the block.

"Gas fumes are heavier than air. They would be collecting in the bottom of the compartment. And let's say these conditions have existed for a while, things have been building up. Today the guy gets in, he's in a hurry. He doesn't open the engine compartment and take a good sniff to make sure there are no leaks, no fumes— hell, he's only going a few hundred yards. He just loosens the lines, drops into the boat, and hits the starter switch. Boom. That's all she wrote."

"And if you were someone interested in sending Gregory Mouton into the great beyond?" asked Ray.

"Piece of cake, Ray. If the perp wanted to go to a lot of trouble, he could sever the fuel line or loosen a fitting, and just pull the lead from the coil to the distributer off and position it so there'd be a good spark when someone tried to start the engine. That said, most of the perps I've encountered in these kinds of things aren't into heavy lifting. My guess is that they'd bring some gas in a water bottle or big gulp cup and pour it in. Then they'd position an ignition wire to produce the needed spark. Voilà! Kaboom! Crude and effective."

"But...?"

"I know what you're thinking." Ogden pointed at the boat. "This is all I've got to work with. Like I said, I'll take some samples and test for other explosives. I doubt if I'll find anything. If you have the resources, you can have your dive team search the bottom for any bits and bobs that weren't consumed by the fire and find a wooden boat guy to help reconstruct what's left of the wreckage."

"Resources," laughed Ray. "One of our county commissioners wants to know why we have a road patrol."

"Where's your right-hand assistant?" asked Ogden.

"She's gone for a few days."

"Pity. I was looking forward to seeing her. By the way, is she dating anyone?"

"She has been, but I have a feeling the relationship isn't going anywhere," said Ray. He much preferred Ogden over the Chicago lawyer Sue had been seeing in recent months. He pointed back at the wreckage. "What should I do with this?"

"Put this wreck on a flatbed trailer. Tuck it into a corner of the county garage for safekeeping on the off chance that we want to take a second look. If either of us comes up with anything suspicious, we'll have a conversation on what to do next."

As Ray started to walk up the hill, Ogden called him back.

"Just a thought. See if you can find anyone who worked on this boat, like the place he was taking it. They might be able to tell you about what shape it was in and the likelihood of the boat going up in flames by accident."

26

Ray retrieved Simone from the Jeep and walked south along the water to the Cedar Bay Boat Works. He found Clark Montgomery, the owner of the business, working on an outboard engine attached to a scruffy pontoon boat that had seen better days.

As Ray approached, Clark slowly pulled himself off a stool, holding onto the side of the boat for support as he worked to straighten his tall frame. After wiping the grease from his weathered hands, he extended the right one in Ray's direction.

"Sheriff, that a new deputy you got with you? You should get your friend a vest and a badge."

"How are you today, Clark?" asked Ray.

"Not so good, Ray. This getting old is a bitch. I'd tell you to avoid it, but, well, you know." He waved off in the direction of the marina. "And seeing that boat go, I can't put it in words."

"Where were you?"

"Right down there," he looked toward the water at the end of the paving. "We were waiting for him. Had the crane in place. I saw him over there on the dock near his boat. Then a few minutes later there was a big bang. Me and the boys, we grabbed some fire extinguishers and ran over in the pickup to see what we could do. We were spraying the area before the fire truck arrived. He musta had it close to full when it blew, fire on the water. Boat was down to the waterline in a couple of minutes. Dock was starting to go, too. I've been working at this since I was a kid, and I've never seen anything like it before. If there's a good thing, that poor SOB never knew what hit him. When it blew, you could feel it in the ground."

"Was Mouton a regular customer?"

"No. This was the first time we were storing his boat for the winter. He always did it himself, trailering it back up to his place for the winter. Came by a few days ago to check on how much it would cost. Said it was getting to be just too much of a hassle for him."

"Had you done other work for him?"

"He started coming around a coupla years ago about the time he began restoring that boat. He'd come down here, bring his father along most times. His father seemed to need some looking after. He was pretty frail and seemed to be failing a bit." Clark pointed to his head with his forefinger. "Greg was searching for parts and information. I could tell the man was over his head right from the beginning.

"I even went up to his place to have a look at the boat when they were just beginning. It was in rough shape, lots of rot in the bottom and some damage to the engine compartment. Greg said at one point they had started on a rebuild and then didn't get back to it. Lots of parts had gone missing. Anyway, I sold them caulk and finishes and some of the mechanical parts over a couple of years. I could tell it was going to be a bodge job, but it wasn't for me to say. Then I didn't see Greg again till this past June. Now that's our busiest time. He'd put his boat in at the marina and couldn't get it started. He wanted me to go over there and work on it. I told him we don't do that. He'd have to get it over here, and we'd probably want to pull it out of the water and bring it into the shed. He got kinda huffy. I reminded him that when he had trouble with his car, he had to take it to the garage. I didn't think I'd see him again.

"A couple days later he's back wanting me to find out what's wrong. We towed it over, got it inside, and started to go through it. The reason it wasn't starting was that all the ignition wires were rotten, leaking juice, so he's not getting enough spark. As soon as I put a new wiring set on, the engine fired right up. But while I was at it, I had a good look around. Like I expected, it was just a total bodge job. The gas tank was rusty. I know it was original. Think about that, Ray, a seventy-plus years-old gas tank. When I mentioned it, he said it wasn't leaking so they didn't replace it. To make matters worse, he had added an electric fuel pump. When I asked him why, he said the mechanical one wasn't delivering enough fuel. Ray, that man knew just enough to be dangerous, real dangerous."

"Clark, Greg's sister was murdered last week, you probably saw it on the news. Now he's dead. I need to know if this was an accident or something staged to look like one."

Montgomery pulled at his chin and looked out at the water. "There were a lot of problems with that boat. And people don't understand the differences between their cars and their boat. The marine environment is completely different. A boat like that, properly maintained, is perfectly safe as it was originally designed and manufactured. But it has to be maintained at a high level. People are used to letting their cars go to hell. Nothing much happens. Maybe you end up at the side of the road occasionally. You do that with a boat, and you can have a tragedy on your hands."

"And if you wanted to sabotage a boat?"

"One of those old ones," he looked in the direction of the marina, "fumes and a spark. And with not much left, I think it would be impossible to tell if it was sabotage or an accident. But I can take a look."

"Thank you. I need the boat stored in a secure spot."

"We could do that," said Montgomery. "Back in one of the old sheds. Locked up and out of sight. Won't cost the county nothing."

27

Ray was inspecting the contents of the refrigerator when he heard a tinny version of the opening of Mahler's Second Symphony echoing from his phone. By the time he found it on the counter under a stack of mail he had carried in a few minutes before, the call was gone. A minute later the phone rang again.

"Did you just call?" he asked, seeing Hanna Jeffers' photo on the screen.

"Yes. I was going to leave you a message, but I have this vision etched in my brain of you frantically looking for the phone. And since I really wanted to talk to you now...."

"You're getting to know me too well."

"How many times have I watched you looking for your phone? I just imagined you were following the same script. What are you doing?"

"Looking for inspiration in an empty fridge so I can avoid the grocery store. How was your day?" asked Ray. "Flight okay?"

"The first one into Minneapolis was a little bumpy over the lake. The second one, well once you get airborne you're in final approach for Rochester. We caught a limo, got checked into our hotel, and made Sue's first appointment on time."

"How did that go?" asked Ray.

"Not what I expected, but good. Sue's first appointment was with an internist in women's medicine. Sue wanted me to stay with her, so I did. I think the physician initially thought we were a couple.

Ray, I've never seen such a thorough intake exam or anyone do such a complete history."

"What about the lump?"

"I'm getting there. The internist, a tall woman by the name of Dr. Baden, had a bit of an accent. Her degrees were on the wall, Heidelberg University, Ph.D. from Stanford. It was a humbling experience to watch her. I've been so specialized for so long I think I've forgotten how to look at the whole person."

"The lump?"

"After she did a complete history and exam, she checked both breasts and the surrounding areas that sometimes contain breast tissue. By this time she understood that I was a physician, too. Ray, I didn't know a lump on a shoulder might be breast cancer, also."

"So Sue's got…?"

"No, Baden was just explaining that the examination has to cover more than just the breasts, the part that rides in the bra. Breast tissue is found in a much broader area. Later, Sue was seen in the breast clinic. Tomorrow morning she will have a biopsy, and we will quickly know what we're dealing with. There's one more thing."

"What's that?"

"Going back to Dr. Baden, during the exam she found something on Sue's back that she didn't like. There's a mole that would normally be under a strap for a bra or swimming suit. So right after the biopsy tomorrow, she has an appointment in dermatology. And then there's the question of genetic testing."

"You're losing me."

"You heard Sue mention that there was a history of breast cancer in her family. She asked me about this when we were on the plane, and it came up during the exam. Sue is wondering if she should have the genetic testing. But she's frightened of learning the results. What if she tests positive? Does she go ahead with the prophylactic surgery, the removal of her breasts? Ray, these are big life issues."

"I don't know what to say," he responded.

"As soon as Sue gets back from the health club, we're going to get a good dinner and a very special bottle of wine."

Ray could hear some background noise, voices, then Hanna said, "Sue's back. I'll pass the phone to her."

"Hey, Ray, how's the investigation?"

"How are you?" he asked, ignoring her question.

"Things are okay. I'm sure Hanna filled you in, probably better than I could have. I'm glad she's with me. What about the investigation?"

Ray explained all the events of the day, starting with the column of black smoke he spotted as he drove north after dropping them at the airport.

"It all sounds pretty grim. Mouton seemed to be a really nice man. Are you okay?"

"I'm glad I've got Simone to worry about tonight."

"You talk to Mouton's wife?"

Ray told her about visiting Sherry Mouton. "The only comfort I could offer was that he was killed instantly, he felt no pain. Some comfort, huh?"

"Was she alone?"

"Yes. Before I left I walked her over to the neighbors. They were working in the yard. The woman immediately took Sherry in her arms. I explained what had happened. The man said they would look after her."

"Tough duty. Sorry I wasn't there."

"Simone's okay," said Ray, moving to change the topic. "After I find something for us to eat, we're off for a walk before it gets too dark."

"Ray, Simone has something to eat. I packed extra cans of food. I'm sure she would share."

28

Sue called Ray the next afternoon just as he was preparing to leave the office.

"Where are you?" he asked.

"I'm in my hotel room."

"Where's Hanna?"

"She's on an art tour. The clinic has an amazing collection spread through several of the buildings. I dropped out and came back here. I thought I'd nap, but as soon as I hit the bed, I was wide-awake thinking about the investigation. What's happening?"

"Not much here. Investigators are still working on the boat explosion. Now I need to know about you."

"Between appointments I ran down Gillian's first husband, Benson Banard III. He lives in Vail, Colorado."

"How did that go?"

"He was aware of her death, her lawyer contacted him. They've been divorced for more than 12 years. He said they met in Vail and had a whirlwind romance. She was in an MBA program at Michigan and he moved to Ann Arbor when they married. He said that going into the marriage there was an understanding that they would move back to Vail when she completed her degree. But by that time she had become fascinated with international business. He said he was a bit older and wanted a family, and she was focused on career, so they went their separate ways. There were no hard feelings on either side."

"So how did it work out for him?"

"He has a wife and three children under twelve. He said he hadn't seen or talked to her in years. He added that there was much to admire about Gillian. He couldn't imagine anyone wanting to harm her. I've done some checking. He seems to be a solid citizen.

"As to my day, long and tiring. Appointments kept getting added to my schedule. I had a mammogram, had two more consultations in the breast clinic, and then they did the lumpectomy. The pathology report will be available tomorrow or the next day. I missed my dermatology visit because of the added appointments. I was hoping we'd be getting out of here in the morning, but Hanna says we aren't leaving until I see the dermatologist. Maybe we can catch a plane before the end of the day. Either way, we'll be home by the weekend. The bad news for you is Hanna is working all weekend. What's the next step?" Sue asked.

"I'm going back to talk to Phillip Lovell. I want a complete tour of the place."

"Think he will cooperate?"

"I don't know, but we need to keep the pressure on him. Let him know he's still a primary suspect. Gillian was looking for something. We need to find out what it was."

29

Ray's attempt to enter the Ursidae Winery and look for Phillip Lovell on his own was hindered near the main entrance by one of the corps of uniformed hosts and guides.

"Sir, do you want to join a tour group, a tasting group, enter our retail store?" the twenty-something woman asked with a forced smile as she blocked his forward progress.

"I need a word with Mr. Lovell," he responded, holding out his ID. She looked at it carefully, studying the photo, and then looking at Ray as if to affirm that he was indeed the person in the photo. "I'll have to check and see if he's available. Please wait here."

Ray watched as she slid behind a counter and lifted a phone. Ray focused on her facial expressions and body language. The woman continued to look at him as she talked on the phone. The buzz of voices in the crowded room prevented him from hearing any of her conversation.

When the woman returned to Ray's side, she said in an officious tone, "I'll guide you to Mr. Lovell's office."

Lovell was on his feet as soon as Ray entered the office, walking around his desk to shake hands. He held on to Ray's hand as he said, "I want to apologize for my rude behavior the other day, Sheriff Elkins. I was upset and not thinking straight. Please have a seat."

Lovell looked toward the young woman still standing near Ray. "Would you get us a fresh flask of coffee. Close the door on your way out."

"You have to understand, Sheriff, I was extremely upset, and I allowed my emotions to push me towards a paranoia of sorts. I would like to make amends for my boorish behavior. How can I be of service?"

"Sir, as far as we know, other than her killer, you were the last person to see Gillian alive."

Before Lovell could respond, there was a knock on the door, and the coffee arrived. After the woman departed, Lovell took his time pouring two mugs of coffee. "That's probably true, based on what you've told me." He paused for a moment as he added some cream to his coffee and stirred it slowly. "Sheriff, I have heard from members of staff who are locals that at the end of the day you always get your man or woman. I applaud your diligence. I have hardly slept a wink since this all happened. I can't imagine I know anything that will help, but please ask away. I am an open book. I have nothing to hide."

"Tell me about your relationship with Gillian Mouton."

"Not much to tell, really. She's been big news for the last three or four years. A breath of fresh air, really, in an industry that can be a bit stodgy. It's not that women weren't buying wine before, but Gillian made it hip and got women drinking better wines at higher price points. This is always good for the industry, the more the consumer knows, the better wine they buy. Have you checked out her website?"

"I've only looked at it briefly," answered Ray.

"Her target audience was professional women, but lots of men use it, too. She made wine accessible and fun."

"How did you get to know her?" asked Ray.

"Actually, I was introduced to her four or five years ago and continued to run into her at international wine events in recent years."

"So how did Gillian's event at Ursidae Winery come about?"

"I ran into her at a wine show in New York this winter. When she noticed that I was now working in northern Michigan, she took a great interest in me. She went on a bit about all the wonderful things that she had heard about Ursidae, that we were producing great wines that were just starting to be discovered. All of that is true, Sheriff, but her enthusiasm seemed a bit over the top. So the long and short of it is that she suggested we cooperate on an event. She was sure that we could pull a large crowd from the Midwest.

"And she was absolutely correct. The event was sold out in less than twenty-four hours, and cancelling it was a job and a half. I can't imagine why, given the circumstances, but so many of those holding reservations were very unhappy with us. We provided a full refund, offered vouchers for free winery tours, and discounts on all our premium wines. I know that people had booked flights and hotels, but the poor woman was dead, for God's sake. What could we do?"

"You said something to the effect that you and Gillian had been having a…casual affair…I think that's how you phrased it."

"Not trying to speak ill of the dead, and I'm glad your sergeant isn't here, these things are easier, man to man."

"Make your point, please," said Ray, growing impatient.

"A casual affair is probably an overstatement. We had a series of one-night stands. Our relationship was about sex, and perhaps loneliness, and business. With Gillian it was always about business. And she was willing to use whatever means necessary…if you know what I mean…to get what she wanted." He gave Ray a weak smile. "Our assignation last Wednesday, that was all engineered by Gillian. We had a planning meeting here and had arranged to connect later in town for dinner. But as we were starting to go our separate ways, she told me about one of the chévres she had picked up from the goat lady, Blythe Erickson. Gillian though it might be a bit too ripe for the uninitiated palates of some of the women. She was looking for the perfect wine from our range to tone it down a bit. She suggested that I follow her to her condo to work out this vexing detail. I offered some feeble excuse about having things to do, but quickly ended up following her. At the end of the day I was falling into one of Gillian's larger agendas, but in the heat of the moment, who cares."

"What was the larger agenda?" asked Ray.

"I'm not sure, but Gillian was after something. You know how she first got national recognition in this business, Sheriff?"

"No."

"It was only, what, four or five years ago. There was a small vineyard out in Napa Valley owned by a couple of dentists. They specialized in Cabernet Sauvignon." Lovell paused for a moment, offering Ray more, then refilling his own coffee mug. "I can't remember exactly what vintage it was, perhaps 2006 or 2007. The wine in question had been in bottles for a few years and was suddenly taking lots of prizes and getting 90 plus ratings on all the major lists. So hold on to this part, Sheriff—a small winery, small number of cases available, and suddenly a huge demand.

"One of the things you learn in this business is that very rich people—whether they're Yanks, Brits, Kiwis, Russian oligarchs, or Chinese billionaires—want to drink what other very rich people are drinking. When money no longer matters, the price goes through the ceiling. This Cab was going for more than a grand wholesale. Add a few bob more for retail, another 150 to 200 percent for restaurants. Well, you get the picture.

"Gillian was familiar with this winery. She had visited it early on and had been tracking the prices of its vintages. Something didn't seem right to her. She started making phone calls, checking on availability from major distributors. Once Gillian figured out that there was about three times more of this pricy vintage available in the system than was ever produced, she set about finding out how the scam had been pulled off.

"Gillian broke the story on her wine blog. The story was quickly picked up by the *Wall Street Journal*, the *New York Times,* and the other major news outlets. Of course, it was headline news in all the trade publications as well. That story really put Gillian's wine newsletter on the map. The people she exposed referred to her as *the wine bitch,* which she then adopted as her trademark."

"The winery, how did they come up with the additional wine?" asked Ray.

"Not so hard. They had other vintages in stock. Some skillful blending from inventory, some bottling, some relabeling with the correct vintage and voilà, more product suddenly appears. It wasn't that Gillian's discovery was totally remarkable. There were suspicions at the wholesale level. But who is going to kill the goose that lays golden eggs?"

"Do you think Gillian thought you were up to a similar kind of mischief?" asked Ray. He held back for a minute and then said, "We've gone over her photos. I think she may have come through as a tourist without identifying herself. There were lots of shots of the interior of your production area, including photos of your security system, like she was casing the place. She also took pictures of the exterior. She seemed very interested in your collection of shipping containers." Ray watched Lovell closely as he delivered the information.

"Doesn't surprise me," Lovell responded. "I had heard that Gillian was desperately short of cash, subscribers to all the major wine lists dropped dramatically during the recession. She needed another big story to get her in the news again. This time she was woofing up the wrong tree."

"Where would she get that idea, something going on here?" asked Ray.

"Lord only knows what you might hear though the grapevine, no pun intended. Indeed, maybe you've heard some of the rumors going around. My favorite is Ursidae is owned by the Russian mafia. These thugs intend to buy up all the area vineyards. Another rumor is that we don't make any of our own wine. It's all shipped in from South Africa, we just bottle it. It goes on and on, Sheriff.

"The problem is that we have a very different business model. Well, that's not the first problem. The first problem is that we're not local. Our great-great-grandparents didn't settle the area. And then we have a very different business model. We are not a small family business. We are part of a multinational corporation that involves the production and distribution of wines and spirits in most of the world's major markets.

"Our friends up and down this peninsula have a vineyard, a winery, and a tasting room. We do also. That said, our winery is much larger and state-of-the-art. We have a huge capacity. We produce some wines from our own vineyards. I'm talking about our Ursidae Estate Wines. These are handcrafted, vintage wines—the labels and corks carrying the year of production. We bring in top international winemakers to help with the blending of these products. And the production of these superior wines is quite limited. We're working to create a scarcity. At this point we're aiming at the $20 to $50 market and expect the prices to go much higher. You can go to our website and see how many cases of each of our estate wines were produced. You can also check our current inventory. We're being proactive, preventing any possible scandal that would damage our reputation.

"But, Sheriff, our estate wines, if that's all we did, our production facilities would be sitting idle for eleven months of the year. Unlike the other producers in the region, we work from a completely different paradigm. This is a highly automated 24/7, 365 days a year production facility.

"In addition to our estate wines, we make two other lines intended to sell at more modest price points. One is made from grapes we buy from this region and across the state. These are marketed as Michigan Heartland Table Wines, great wines for less than ten bucks. They are something you pick to go with dinner, an enjoyable wine at a good price.

"Our entry product line, American Eagle Table Wines, is made from juice that we process here or buy from other sources. It's not great wine, it's a commodity, only a fiver or less. But at the end of the day it's much better than Two-Buck Chuck. It's a beverage that's crafted to the tastes of wine drinkers in the Midwest. And since we're not shipping it across the country, we can put the quality in the beverage, not in the cost of bringing it here.

"Now there have been some nasty rumors floating around that all of our wine is one and the same. The only differences are the labels and prices. So I go back to your question, why was Gillian here? Was this possibly her next big scoop? I don't think so. Gillian had impeccable taste. She was a true connoisseur, could spot a fraud a mile off. She wouldn't have bought that story."

"Surely, you must have some idea what she was after?" pressed Ray.

"I don't know. As you see, there's nothing here." He paused for a long moment. "Unless she was playing with the idea of doing a piece that pits companies like mine against the small producers. You know, traditional ways and values under siege by heartless, international conglomerates. Maybe she thought she could create a sentimental spin on how this bucolic world—Geppetto and the folksy winemakers—was about to be seized and destroyed, their perfect terroir stolen away by an evil other. She might have been able to get some mileage on that. Sheriff, I need to show you this place, so you know what I'm referring to. I take it you've seen the workings of some of the other wineries?"

"Yes," said Ray.

After a lengthy tour—starting with grapes being loaded into the crushers and ending in the bottling plant, where bottles were sanitized, filled, labeled, sealed, and loaded in cardboard cases— they emerged at the rear of the facility.

"I bet you've never seen this level of technology at the other wineries," gloated Lovell.

"Never," agreed Ray. "Most impressive." He pointed at the shipping containers on a paved area some distance from the plant. "Tell me about those. Are you exporting?"

"Why don't we walk over," urged Lovell. "I'll show you."

Lovell opened the doors of the first container. "As you can see, thousands of new bottles for our premium wines. We get them directly from France by the container load."

"How about the other containers?" asked Ray.

"Let's check them out," said Lovell. One by one he opened the next four containers. "As you can see, Sheriff, they are all filled with new bottles."

"What happens when the containers are empty?"

"They get picked up by the freight expediter."

"You're not filling them with wine for the international market?"

"Not yet," answered Lovell. "But it's something I want to accomplish before I move on to my next position. It would be a real plus on my résumé. Our wine is good enough to do well in the international market. We just need more exposure."

Lovell looked around, and then turned to Ray. "Lovely fall day, isn't it. If it weren't for the harsh winters, I could see spending a life here. Is there anything else, Sheriff? "

"Not at the moment. You've been very generous with your time. Thank you."

"If I can be of further assistance, please don't hesitate to call."

"Come to think of it, there is one more thing. Do you have any thoughts about why Gillian Mouton ended up in one of Terroir Nord's vineyards?"

"I shouldn't say anything, really…."

Ray waited.

"At that wine show in New York, one of the Donaldson's sons was hanging around Gillian's booth. Sort of peculiar, if you know what I mean. He looked like he was in heat, and she seemed to be stoking the fire a bit. She was a tease."

"Which brother?"

"I couldn't tell you. The twins, doppelgangers. Hope that helps, Sheriff. The poor woman deserves justice."

30

For much of the evening Ray sat at the kitchen table and keyed a draft of the incident report on the death of Gregory Mouton. Working from extensive notes, he provided an account of everything that was currently known. He included information from expert witnesses, including Mike Ogden of the Michigan State Police and Clark Montgomery, owner of the Cedar Bay Boat Works. Ray also summarized his conversation with Sherry Mouton, wife of the deceased, and noted that interviews and canvassing by his deputies had failed to produce any witnesses who had seen someone other than Mouton near the boat the night before or the morning of the explosion. At the end Ray appended Mike Ogden's preliminary report. After completing the draft, he printed a hard copy and read it out loud, making notes in the margin for further revision. Then he entered the changes and did a final proofing.

Next Ray turned his attention to his interview with Phillip Lovell. He carefully outlined their conversation and what he observed during his tour of the winery. Ray's account was a straight recitation of the facts. He was always mindful that these documents might be carefully read by a defense attorney at some later date.

Finally, he wrote up his conversation with Blythe Erickson. Then Ray added the Lovell and Erickson interviews to the Gillian Mouton folder.

After completing the final draft, he took Simone for her last walk of the day. He had pulled on an old down jacket and, as Simone dallied, exploring the scents and sounds of an autumn eve, he stopped and pulled up the zipper, closing out the cool breeze, a harbinger of the harsh winter that was rapidly approaching.

Before retiring, Ray turned his attention to his journal. Now he was freed from the tight restrictions of police reports. He was able to lay out the sensory details, gut feelings, and personal biases.

Ray filled a fountain pen and then carefully wiped the ink off the grip. Sliding the barrel back into the cap, he looked at the instrument for a long moment, the shiny black surface, the polished gold of the nib. He loved the feel of the pen in his hand and the tactile sensation as he moved the pen over the paper, spreading lines of brown ink over the tan pages. And then there was the sound, the subtle scratching noise as the tip accelerated, decelerated and paused in the process of forming words and adding punctuation.

He wrote the words, *Phillip Lovell,* then paused a long moment, putting himself in Lovell's office earlier in the day. Ray started with smell, Lovell's smell—the cloying odor of too much perfume or aftershave, perhaps a combination of the two. Next he wrote about Lovell's manner—his ingratiating tone, without a hint of the anger and hostility that was so apparent at the end of their last encounter. Ray also noted that Lovell was often flushed during the course of their encounter, several times wiping away perspiration with a handkerchief.

So while his outward appearance and manner suggested bonhomie, Ray wrote, *the gloss of sweat suggested something else, an inner tension. Lovell went out of his way to show me everything, including the shipping containers. Was this all a setup? Had everything been carefully staged in the anticipation of my visit? Was Lovell involved in the death of Gillian Mouton? Perhaps. If he wasn't, what other kind of scam might he be running? Is he stealing from the company, cheating on taxes, being less than truthful about his products?*

Next Ray turned his attention to Blythe Erickson and their late afternoon hillside conversation over herbal tea. Blythe reminded him of so many other refugees to Cedar County, usually skilled and educated people who walk away from good jobs in the cities and come north with the dream of living in a beautiful corner of the world. Since there are few employment opportunities locally, these people scramble to make a living. Many survive through hard work and persistence, continuing to reinvent themselves as necessary, finding ways to eke out enough of a living to sustain their dream. Others burn out, become discouraged, and wander back to the cities after they have depleted their nest eggs.

Blythe appears to have the passion to make this venture go. With a bit of luck she should be successful. The path she has chosen is filled with hard work and probably modest rewards, but it puts her where she wants to be, at least for the moment.

I wish I could have seen Blythe and Gillian together. I suspect it would have been a study in contrasts. Blythe is trying to build a life at the edge of the economy. By contrast, Gillian was at the center of an international business.

Ray turned to the phone call he had received from Sue a few hours earlier. She would be returning for the weekend, perhaps with the pathology reports in hand. Then they could plan for the immediate future, whatever that might be.

His hand hovered over the page. He wrote one word, *Cancer.* Then he stood for a long period, not wanting to continue. He thought about his father, a heavy drinker and smoker. About a year before his death, he had started to experience intense pain in his right arm. By the time he had sought medical help, he had advanced metastatic disease, and there were no treatments available other than palliative care. Ray reflected on his mother's last illness, breast cancer. For her, it was just one more of the diseases of old age winnowing her away.

Then he thought about Ellen, his long-time companion, who died of cancer more than a decade before, one of the events that contributed to his move north to start another life. He had never fully recovered from Ellen's death and had struggled with relationships after her passing. Ray always felt he was holding back, never quite able to fully commit again. Hanna's recent question about their being a couple had reawakened some of that discomfort. Then he thought about Hanna considering a job at Stanford. This all brought Ray back to a comment by a grief counselor at the time of Ellen's death talking about the childhood fears of abandonment that many people carry into adulthood. He wondered how much that was part of his psyche.

And then he thought about Sue and how important she was to his life. He looked back at the last word he had written, *Cancer,* standing alone at the top of a yet unwritten paragraph, and he remembered a few lines from Hemingway:

"In the swamp fishing was a tragic adventure. Nick did not want it. He did not want to go down the stream any farther today."

He carefully replaced the cap on the pen and returned it and the journal to their storage places in his writing desk.

31

Ray found Clark Montgomery reclining in a battered wooden office chair in his small, littered office at the Cedar Bay Boat Works.

"Want some coffee? You look like you need it. Just made it fresh."

"Sure," Ray answered.

Montgomery picked an empty mug off the shelf, carefully eyed the interior, took a wipe at something with his index and middle finger, and then filled the cup.

As he passed the coffee to Ray, he said, "If you want sugar or cream, you're out of luck."

"No, this is perfect."

"Having trouble sleeping?" Montgomery asked.

"Lots going on," answered Ray.

"Wait till you get old," said Montgomery. "Last time I saw my doc I mentioned the sleep thing. SOB gave me the same old answer I'm so tired of hearing, 'It's just an age-related problem.' Maybe to him that's all it is. There's a 40-something guy who's not dragging his ass all day because he had a good night's sleep. But to me, it's a hell of a problem, age-related or not."

"I got your message. So what's this about a spark plug?" asked Ray.

"As soon as I have a little more of my coffee," said Montgomery.

Finally, Ray followed Montgomery out the large door of the steel building that opened to the lakefront. They stopped near the far side of a paved area and Montgomery pulled a blue tarp off the remains of Gregory Mouton's boat.

"We had it sitting in the sun, Ray. Wanted to get it dried out and all the fumes evaporated away before we put it undercover. I was down here late yesterday before closing to check on it. I wanted to get it covered in case it rained. That's when I noticed the spark plug." Montgomery pointed, "It's right there laying under the starter motor." He reached in, grabbed it, and held it out to Ray.

"Look at the engine. All the plugs are in place. The boots and wires are mostly gone. I imagine the force of the explosion, the intense fire, and the force of the spray from the high-pressure hoses all contributed to that. But if you look closely, the spark plug terminals, the pieces that go at the end of the plug wire and attach to the terminals on the top of the plugs, they're all in place 'cept for the number three cylinder.

"Someone pulled that wire off the three plug in the engine, attached it to the one in your hand, and placed it in the bottom of the boat. The first time Greg hit the ignition, boom. And I bet the person who did it never dreamed it would end up staying there. And the plug is interesting, too."

"How's that?"

"That's not a marine plug. It's not even a four-cycle plug."

"Well, what is it, then?" Ray was getting impatient at the pace of the conversation.

"That's for a lawn mower, probably an old Lawn Boy two-cycle."

"How do you know this?"

"We got one in the shed, must be thirty, forty years old. Keep the weeds down with it during the summer."

"Have you checked to see if it's missing a spark plug?"

"That's the first thing that hit me. I went and checked. The plug is right where it's supposed to be."

"So what do you think, someone bought a plug and...?"

"No, not quite like that. You got a low budget thug on the loose."

"What do you mean?"

"Ray, look at the plug. It sure ain't new. The electrode is worn away. You can probably find old plugs in half the garages and barns in the county. It's the kind of thing guys throw in a drawer or on a bench. Don't know what their thinking is, not likely they'll ever use them again."

"Tell me what you think happened."

"Whoever did this, they came with that spark plug you got in your hand. After opening the doors to the engine compartment, they pulled the lead off the number three spark plug and attached it to the one there. They placed that in the bottom of the boat and poured in some gasoline. Wouldn't need much, only takes a cup or two. And they might have used a lot more. Wouldn't have taken long for fumes to fill the whole compartment. That would have been like having several sticks of dynamite waiting for a spark. Greg comes to get his boat. He doesn't open and check the engine compartment for fumes. He just jumps in, hits the ignition. End of story."

"You're pretty sure about this?"

"Absolutely. But if you want to check for sure, just get the State Police guy to compare the terminals. They will all be the same. These things change little over the years. He won't find no differences. You're looking for a killer, Ray. No doubt about it now."

"How about Gregory Mouton? What if he wanted to off himself?"

"Now there's a thought. Didn't think about that possibility. But then I don't know much about Greg. So, like I said, you got either a killer or a suicide. Wouldn't have suspected him for that, the suicide part, but what do I know. I'll stick with marine engines and let someone else do the head shrinking."

32

On Friday, Sue arrived at Ray's office midmorning for a case review. "I know I said, 'thank you,' last night. But I need to say it again. Sorry you had to spend the evening at the airport waiting."

"It wasn't so bad," Ray answered. "I had an array of recent *New Yorkers* on my iPad that I hadn't gotten to. And from time to time Simone and I explored the perimeter of the parking area. Lots of interesting smells, sights, and sounds, especially in the shadowy areas. It's probably the most interesting evening she's had in a long time."

"I'd been hearing about 'flights from hell' from my friends," said Sue. "Now I fully comprehend what they were bitching about."

After organizing some materials on the conference table, she continued, "I imagine Hanna brought you up-to-date on the pathology. I know she was reluctant to say anything, sort of invoking the doctor/patient relationship. I told her that she could explain things better to you than I can."

"Hanna told me the breast biopsy was negative. But the birthmark...."

"Yes. Strange, I was carrying something around that could be very deadly. Who looks at their back?"

"So what do you know?"

"The dermatologist, a young guy not much older than me, said while the site was still small, he thought it had the appearance of a superficial spreading melanoma. He brought in several of his colleagues to look at it. And after much conversation, it was decided that instead of just doing a biopsy, they would remove it and a big chunk of the surrounding tissue. Of course, the docs didn't say it quite like that, but essentially that was their meaning. The long and short of it is that I should hear something today. They want me to come back in a few weeks for some more tests to make sure they got it all. Ray, I think I really was lucky. I went to Rochester scared to death about breast cancer only to find that I probably had another form of cancer. Part of me is relieved, part is scared. If I hadn't found the lump, the melanoma wouldn't have been discovered anytime soon." Sue paused for a long moment. "This was a real awakening. I've always been as healthy as a horse. As you know, I'm seldom sick. Then suddenly there's the specter of breast cancer, followed by skin cancer. This has brought my own mortality into focus. I liked it better when I was going to live forever."

Ray didn't respond verbally. He just held her in his gaze and nodded.

"So bring me up to speed on Gregory Mouton. I've read the reports, fill in the blanks," said Sue.

"I think now there is every reason to believe that this wasn't an accident. It might have been a murder, but there is also the possibility of suicide. There was an extra spark plug, the wrong type for the boat, lying next to the keel. It appears that a wire had been pulled off one of the plugs in the engine and attached to the extra plug. If Clark hadn't found it and called our attention to it…well, the accident scenario…."

"According to the incident report, you had the area canvassed and no one saw anything."

"That's right, but someone could have tampered with the Chris Craft during the night. This time of year not much is happening after 11:00 or so. Except for Mouton's boat, the marina was empty."

"How about your interview with Sherry Mouton?"

"You saw my notes. Sherry was rather convincing in the role of the shocked, grieving widow. Now we need to take a second look. We need to talk to Sherry again. I think that would be a good thing for you to do. Or maybe we should team?"

"That would be good, and I'd like to see what we can find out about each of them— personal, financial. For some reason I want to believe that she's not involved, but let's give her a hard look."

Ray went silent.

"What are you thinking?" asked Sue.

"I was sort of distracted. I dropped the ball on Gregory's death and focused on Gillian. And now we're dealing with two murders," said Ray.

"Tell me about your encounter with Phillip Lovell. Your notes were very guarded."

"Yes, guarded. I can just see a defense attorney reading from my notes at trial. Something like, 'Suspect seemed unusually oily.'"

"Was he oily?"

"He was just too cooperative. And since you weren't there, we had a man-to-man talk about Gillian."

"I'm sitting at the edge of my seat waiting for the sizzling details."

"Sorry, I can't rat out my good chum by sharing this private conversation."

"What can you tell me?"

"He put on a good show. He personally gave me a complete tour of the winery. It was very thorough. He made a big point of showing me the shipping containers behind the winery. He insisted that I look in each of them."

"And what did they contain?"

"Bottles, empty bottles, new empty bottles. If there had been anything suspicious around, it had been carefully removed."

"So what are you saying?" asked Sue.

"Gillian had an agenda. And she had a reputation for exposing wine fraud. If Lovell was up to anything, he would have been suspicious of Gillian's motives. We have all of her pics of Ursidae. She was focused on the security system and the shipping containers, so she must have been trying to figure out how she could get in and case the place when no one was around. I think Lovell knew what she was looking for. And whatever that might have been is no longer on the premises."

"Where does that leave us?"

"I wish she had been considerate enough to leave a diary. At this point we should probably get a search warrant for her apartment in New York and her financial records. Do you feel like a trip to New York? Blythe Erickson, the goat lady, says Gillian's apartment is in a very trendy part of Manhattan. You'd probably find it quite interesting."

"I'll talk to her lawyer again, see if she can direct me to Gillian's accountant. I don't want to travel for a few days. Let me see what I can discover electronically. How about Randy Donaldson?"

"I didn't like him. The guy's a liar and a manipulator. Has he ever been on our hit parade?"

"Doesn't ring any bells. I'll check that out," said Sue.

"Okay, see what you can dig up this morning. I'll give Sherry Mouton a call, see if she's planning on being around this afternoon."

33

"Another day in God's country," said Sue as she maneuvered her Jeep out of the parking lot and headed toward the highway.

"Do I detect a hint of sarcasm?" asked Ray.

"Frustration," Sue answered. "We've got one or more killers on the loose, and we're not even close to making an arrest." She stopped at the base of Government Center Drive and waited for the traffic to clear. "Any problem getting Sherry Mouton to talk to us?"

"Not at all. She almost seemed happy that we were coming by," said Ray. "What did you learn about Sherry?"

"She's barely on the radar for anything. Her maiden name was Sherry Ann Kowalski. She graduated from Dondero High in Royal Oak, and she married Gregory Mouton. She doesn't Tweet or do Facebook. It's pretty hard to be invisible these days, but Sherry has managed to do that."

"How about her husband?"

"Lots of things. Not that he did social media, but he was involved in a variety of business and civic activities. He went to State and was active in the Detroit Spartans."

"Any criminal complaints?"

"No." She paused at a stop sign and waited for a casino-bound bus to clear the intersection.

Ray gazed out at the bay. A thin mist floated above the quiet water.

"How are you going to play this?" asked Sue. "Are you going to introduce the possible murder or suicide scenario?"

"I won't lead with that. I'll say something like, 'It appears to be an accident, but with Gillian's murder, we have to look at all possibilities.' I want to give her just enough to keep her ill at ease." He paused briefly. "I also want to have a good look around the barn."

"What are you searching for?"

"I'll ask if we can see the area where Greg and his father did the restoration."

"You didn't answer my question. What are we really looking for?" asked Sue.

"An old lawnmower, the kind you push, with a two-stroke engine. The brand is probably Lawn Boy, and the original color was Kermit green. If she has one, it might be in the garage, the barn, or out behind the barn in the tall grass. If you happen to spot a mower, see if the spark plug is missing."

"How do you know about the tall grass?"

"If you've got an old barn, there's always tall grass on the side facing the back forty. And the tall grass is always filled with junk."

"But these people are from downstate, Birmingham, maybe they—"

"Sue, they all go native in a year or two. Just watch your step. There are probably bicycles, an old tractor, the remains of a pickup truck, and who knows what else. In the winter the junk is hidden by snow. In the summer grass does the trick."

Sherry Mouton was in the yard when they arrived, approaching the Jeep soon after Sue had brought it to a stop.

After they exchanged greetings, Sherry escorted them to the deck at the rear of the house. Glasses and a pitcher of ice tea were already arranged on the picnic table. As they settled in, Sherry asked, "Do you know when his body will be released? I need to arrange for cremation. I'm planning a memorial service here at the house, and I'd like to spread the ashes at the end of the service."

"I'll call you back later today or tomorrow. I can't imagine they will need it much longer," Ray answered.

"I'd appreciate that. I've been getting the house ready. It's given me some focus, so I just don't spend my time falling apart. Thankfully, I've had lots of friends looking in and helping me."

"Do you have children, Mrs. Mouton?" Sue asked.

"No, sadly. We wanted children, but it never happened."

Mouton turned her attention to Ray. "What do you know from the autopsy? On your last visit you were giving me the medical examiner's best guess."

"At this point, I have a preliminary report. The autopsy confirmed the medical examiner's early impressions. Your husband's death was instantaneous. His body sustained major trauma from the explosion."

They sat in silence for several moments. Ray looked over at Sherry. She wiped away some tears, and then said, "We'll spread the ashes out there. Just below the ridge, downhill running toward the swale. He always loved that piece of land. Said it was his favorite place to play as a kid. It was his personal wilderness, the location of so many boyhood adventures. I want Gregory to become one with the place that brought him great happiness.

"I hope I can get this done while we have such a splendid backdrop with the trees in full color. Fall was Gregory's favorite season. It's the perfect time and place to celebrate his life." She paused for a moment, and then asked, "Have you established the cause of the explosion yet?"

"The State Police are helping us with that part of the investigation. They've tested samples taken from the boat for the presence of explosive agents. None were detected. The current theory is that the blast was caused by gasoline fumes. It was probably accidental, but we have to look at all possibilities."

Mouton looked perplexed. "How could it have been anything but an accident? I don't understand?"

"Your sister-in-law was recently murdered, then your husband dies in what appears to be an unfortunate accident. Are these deaths just a tragic coincidence, or is there a connection? My marine consultant says there is always the possibility that someone could have tampered with things to create an explosion. I do need to ask you again if your husband was in any danger. Might Gillian have told him something that put him in harm's way, too?"

"I can't answer that. I sort of stayed out of the way when she was here. The majority of time they spent together was on the boat. I wasn't there."

"Could there be something from the time his business was failing? Maybe an unhappy creditor or disgruntled employee?"

"I don't think so. When we liquidated, our creditors were almost paid in full. And as for employees, at the end, it was just a few old-timers who could have retired years before. They were all friends who were staying on out of loyalty."

"Anything in his personal life?" asked Sue.

"I don't know what you're suggesting."

"Let me give you an example," said Sue. "We've had people come to blows over the location of a new fence. You never know what will trigger violence."

"No, no problems with neighbors. And nothing else, Sergeant. We are very boring people."

"Was your husband dealing with any illness, physical or mental?" asked Ray.

"Not at all, Sheriff. He had adjusted to his new circumstances."

"Mrs. Mouton, you've mentioned your economic struggles. With your husband gone, are you going to be okay?" asked Ray.

"It's a source of worry. We owned this place outright, after we bought out Gillian's part. We'd been putting money in IRAs over the years, but they've taken a big hit the last few years. Greg wasn't happy about it, but I was looking for work. Now that's what I'm going to do. I've run an office before. I can do it again. In truth, at this point I need something to fill my time almost as much as the money."

Ray pointed toward the barn. "That's where they rebuilt the Chris Craft?"

"It went in several stages, Sheriff. The boat was on a trailer. They pulled it out in front of the barn and emptied all the junk that had been tossed in it over the years. Both old Mike and Greg had this 'out of sight, out of mind' approach to cleaning. Then they cleared out the barn after a fashion so they would have a covered work area."

"Is there anything left from the restoration—pictures, diagrams, that sort of thing. I've only seen the wreckage. I really have no idea of what the boat looked like."

"There may be, I don't know. That's always been Greg's place. Why don't we go look?"

Ray and Sue followed Mouton toward the weather-beaten, drooping building.

"Lot of grass here," Ray observed. "Do you have a lawn service?"

"We've got an ancient Gravely tractor with a deck. Greg would mostly do the mowing. In the fall, like now, when his allergies were getting to him, I would take it over."

The central door was pushed open, exposing the largely empty interior.

As they headed in, Sue said, "I'm a bit chilled. I'm going to stay out here in the sun." He gave her a knowing nod.

"If there's anything, it would be on those benches over there." Mouton switched on a bank of fluorescent lights suspended over the work area. Tools littered the top of the bench. At one end was a small stack of books.

"These seem all to be about Chris Crafts," Mouton said, spreading out the books.

Ray paged through the first book slowly, and then looked through several more, stopping at one point and asking, "Is this the boat?"

"Sheriff, they all look about the same. In truth, boats were never my thing. Would you like to take these books with you? You can study them at your leisure."

"Thank you, no. What I'm really looking for are photos taken during or after the restoration."

"Sheriff, if they're not here, they never existed. Gregory didn't throw much away."

They emerged to find Sue standing in a patch of sunlight beyond the shadow of the barn.

"Is this Saab yours?" Ray asked as they neared the house, stopping at the side of a black convertible.

"It's my baby, a reminder of better times. We bought it on a whim. We were able to do things like that back in the day. It was a birthday present." A few minutes later, when Sue and Ray were back on the highway, he asked, "What did you find behind the barn?"

"Two battered and faded lawn mowers, one green, the other grey with some red trim. Both still had spark plugs. There was also a rusting garden tractor. No bikes or pickups. So you weren't exactly right."

"Close enough. The Moutons were still in transition. Maybe they needed another year or two to become permafudge."

34

It was the buzz, the sound of the phone vibrating against the top of the nightstand, as much as the tinny ringtone that pulled Ray from deep sleep.

"This is Central, Sheriff. We've had a 911 from a Mary Donaldson at Terroir Nord Winery. They've had some vandalism in the last few days. Her husband went to check over the property. He hasn't come back, and he's not answering his cell."

"Who's available?" asked Ray, as he looked at the time.

"No one. South sector has a personal injury and north is on a domestic."

"State Police?"

"Not in the county or close."

"I'll go. And I'll need backup. Call Sergeant Lawrence. If she's not available, get someone else." Ray dropped his feet to the floor. "Call Donaldson back. See if she knows what area of their farm Marty was checking on."

Within minutes Ray was rolling south, not turning on the overheads or siren until he reached the highway. Thick fog filled low-lying areas in the cool predawn. Before he reached Terroir Nord Winery, Central was back with his answer. "Ray, the wife says start with the vineyard where the body was found. Backup is rolling."

Ray slowed as the fog thickened, using the dash mounted GPS to keep his bearings—road signs and the terrain all lost in the mist. Finally he found Pelkin Hill Road and started down the rough, washboard surface of the gravel road. Donaldson's pickup was pulled just outside of the entrance to the vineyard, the headlights were on, and the gate was pushed partially open.

Ray parked behind the truck. Memories of his first visit to the vineyard came rushing back. Grabbing a flashlight, he checked the interior of the cab. The engine was still running. Then he turned his attention to the vineyard.

He stood and yelled for Donaldson several times. There was no response. Following the path on the south side of the vineyard, he started up the hill. Pausing on each terrace, he sent the beam between the trellises. Within a few rows Ray spotted Donaldson, face down. He slowly advanced, shining his light beyond the prostrate figure.

In the dirt on the right side of Donaldson's body was a double barrel shotgun. He scanned the body for injuries or blood, then knelt and palpated the soft tissue of Donaldson's neck. Repositioning the tips of his fingers, he continued to probe until he found a slow, thin pulse. He called for an ambulance.

Within minutes the relative quiet of the rural night was shattered by sirens. From his position high on the hill, Ray watched the paramedics arrive, followed by Sue's Jeep. The beams of flashlights and sounds of voices filled the night air. Donaldson was quickly secured to a stretcher and hurriedly moved to the waiting ambulance. Ray and Sue followed, Ray cradling the double-barrel shotgun, now open, in his right hand. The brass heads of two live rounds extended from the breach.

One of Donaldson's boys arrived just as the EMT's were loading his father into the ambulance.

"Randy," said Ray.

"No, I'm Chuck. What's happened?"

"Your father appears to have had a heart attack. You should pick up your mother and drive her to the hospital."

Within minutes Ray and Sue were standing alone, the first hints of the approaching day just beginning to creep over the horizon.

"What was Donaldson doing here," Sue asked. "Why the gun?"

"Mary Donaldson told dispatch that her husband was out checking on an area where they had had some vandalism. I wonder what that's about? They haven't contacted us regarding vandalism."

"Maybe we should head for the hospital and—"

"You head to the hospital, I'll wait for backup," said Ray. "I want this area secured until we can look things over in daylight. Maybe you can get something out of Mary Donaldson."

35

Ray found Sue waiting for him near the entrance to the emergency department, a new monolithic structure grafted to the middle of the medical center. She passed him a tall coffee. "A cappuccino—four shots of espresso and fat free milk."

"You're a lifesaver. I've either got a no-sleep or a low-caffeine headache." He took a modest sip as Sue started to catch him up.

"Donaldson is in the Cardiac Intensive Care Unit. His wife and son have huddled with the doctors a couple of times. I haven't had an opportunity to talk with her yet."

"Just one son?" asked Ray.

"Yes, Chuck. He's not the one you questioned?"

"Correct. And Marty?"

"I had a brief conversation with one of the ER docs. Donaldson has a history of coronary heart disease, and he is currently in serious condition."

"Did he have any other injuries?"

"No."

They settled on some low couches near the intake area. "I would like to talk to Donaldson's wife, get some background on this vandalism. Then I'd like to talk to the son, both sons if Randy shows up. They won't give anything away without being pressured. Maybe with their dad's life in jeopardy, they'll be a bit more cooperative," said Ray.

"I don't know where to begin," said Mary Donaldson, her son Chuck at her side, where they were gathered with Sue and Ray in a small conference room adjacent to the Cardiac Care Unit. "Ever since Marty found that woman's body, our lives have been turned upside down."

Ray looked across the small, sterile room—white walls and ceiling with the one requisite Up North photo (sand dunes running down to brilliant blue water). Mary, in jeans and a shapeless sweatshirt, was collapsed on the plastic cushion of a small couch. Her son was seated next to her in another chair, the armrests touching. Although they had never had a conversation, Ray knew Mary by sight. She was someone he had seen at the local market or on her husband's arm at community events. Under the harsh white light of the fluorescents, she looked worn and defeated.

"Tell me, Mary, what's been going on?"

She remained quiet for a long moment, staring at her Nikes, her focus appearing to be the small hole on the top of the right toe. Slowly lifting her head, she looked directly at Ray. "It's hard to explain, Sheriff. Marty's been a crazy man since that morning he found the body, going on and on about how his vineyard had been violated, that something evil had spread over his grapes. He's just been obsessed, having trouble sleeping, eating. He was convinced that the killer would come back. Somehow he thought that if he could catch the killer he could purify the place." She paused, taking a deep breath, then exhaling heavily. "I was worried, but I thought it would pass, especially after all the grapes were harvested. No such luck. And when he found the vines were cut, for Marty that was almost too much."

"The vines were cut? When did this happen?" asked Sue.

"Thursday, I guess," she said, looking at her son.

"That's right," Chuck Donaldson confirmed. "He found them Thursday morning. I wasn't even up yet. He called me from the vineyard. When I got down there…I've never seen him like that. It was all personal, directed at him."

"I wish you would have called about this. What exactly happened?" said Ray.

"Someone had gone through the vineyard and cut through some of the vines at the trunk. It was crazy, random. A few plants here, a few there, from one end of the vineyard to the other. Looked like they were cut by a small chainsaw, probably battery operated, little or no noise."

"Before Thursday morning, when was the last time he'd been to this vineyard."

"He's been down there a couple of times a day."

"So it happened overnight," Ray said. "Why were we not contacted?" Ray looked directly at Chuck.

"I told him, Sheriff. I told him this was a police matter. But he wouldn't hear of it. He said we could handle this. It would be best not to have the police hanging around. And this is our busy time, so I didn't push it. I thought he'd get beyond it."

After a perfunctory knock, the door opened, and Randy Donaldson entered, escorted by one of the hospital social workers. Randy bent over and hugged his mother, before settling at her side.

"Sorry I wasn't here sooner. I had my phone off. I headed in as soon as I found your message," he said, addressing his mother.

"We'll let you catch up," said Ray. Sue followed him out.

Two blocks away, in the shadows of the old state asylum—a large complex of yellow-brick Victorian buildings that were being converted to apartments and shops—Ray and Sue washed down marzipan croissants with strong coffee in a chichi bakery and coffee shop.

"What's our plan now?" Sue asked.

"We need to separate Mary Donaldson from the boys. I want to put pressure on them. Maybe we can get a bit of the truth. Let me see if Hanna is available," he said, flipping through his contact list.

Twenty minutes later, after Hanna Jeffers escorted Mary Donaldson away to confer about her husband's condition, Ray invited Randy and Chuck to join them at the small table in the center of the room. "You have the latest medical report. Your father is in grave condition, perhaps brought on by his worry and upset over the death of Gillian Mouton." He paused for a long moment. "From the beginning we've had less than your full cooperation. Randy, you failed to mention that you had personally shown Gillian the area where she ended up being murdered hours later.

"Then there's the destruction of some vines in the same vineyard, and no one bothers to call. I don't understand."

"Why would we bother, Sheriff?" asked Randy. "This is our busy season. We're working twelve-hour days. We're exhausted. Making this a police matter would have just wasted three or four hours we didn't have."

"Interesting excuse, Randy, but you are just blowing hot air. We have several sources that say you've known Gillian Mouton several years. That you've been seen in her company at wine shows. Gillian was in that vineyard because you two had something going," said Ray. "You told her to meet you there. Why?"

"Get it over with," urged his brother.

Randy rolled the nails of his right hand against the tabletop three or four times. He looked directly at Ray and said, "I had no plans to meet Gillian."

Sue looked at the other brother, Chuck. "What do we need to know?"

"Don't," said Randy, looking at his brother. "We need a lawyer."

"Come on, Randy. Out with it," said Ray.

"Okay, this is how it happened. The day I took her to see that vineyard, she wanted to know if I had an ATV. When I said yes, she said she had a big favor. Could I get her near the Ursidae Winery late at night? She wanted to have a look around."

"And what did you tell her?"

"I said I could. It wouldn't have been that hard. Chuck and I have been riding all the trails and paths around here since we were kids. We agreed to meet around 9:00. At the time I had really planned to meet her. After we parted, I started thinking that would be a dumb thing to do. They've got a lot of sophisticated security at Ursidae. How would it look if I got caught with Gillian snooping around there? So I didn't show. I thought when she found out I wasn't there, she'd take off. How was I to know something like this would happen?"

"Tell me again where you were that Wednesday night."

"I was running the crusher until around 10:00, then I went home and got cleaned up from a long day."

"You said a high school boy was helping you, a...."

"Shane, Shane Holiday."

"You told me the first time we talked you then went to bed. Is that still your story?"

Randy looked at the ground. "No, I spent the night with my girlfriend."

"Does she have a name?"

"Does she have to be involved?"

"Yes."

"Sheila Nevins, she has a condo at Sugarloaf."

"Chuck, had you ever met Gillian?" asked Sue.

"Never, just read about her and heard some stories from Randy."

"So tell me about the vandalism?" Ray asked Chuck. "What I want to know is motive. Why did this happen? Certainly you've got some theories? Someone's got to be angry with you."

"We can't explain it," said Chuck. "We've thought about it a lot."

36

After parking outside of the entrance to the Terroir Nord vineyard, Sue walked Simone along the edge of Pelkin Hill Road. Ray followed along on the crown of the little used gravel road. As Simone slowly perused the primordial mysteries of the collective scents on a cluster of dandelions, Ray said, "Do you think Randy was telling us the truth?"

"I'll check the names he gave us, see if his alibi holds water. At this point I think he's telling the truth."

"I think I agree."

"The thing I don't quite understand is why Marty Donaldson is obsessing about this. I mean, I understand his being upset about Gillian's murder. But the coming down here at night to check the place over, carrying a shot gun, what was that about?" Sue asked as they turned and started walking back up the road toward her Jeep.

"I've had a slight acquaintance with Marty for years. He's a serious guy, very intense and hard working. I think his wife captured what was going on in Marty's head when she used words like 'violation' and 'evil.' And then his finding some of his vines destroyed...."

"I hear you," said Sue. "We all have things we treasure, and we all have a breaking point." As she lifted Simone into the Jeep, she continued. "Let's have a good look around. I doubt there was anyone around last night, but just in case something was left behind."

A few minutes later they were standing over the spot where Ray had discovered Marty Donaldson.

"No signs of a struggle when you first found Donaldson?" Sue asked.

"I wasn't thinking about that. My focus was seeing if Marty was alive, then getting help. Before the EMTs arrived, I moved the shotgun he must have been carrying. I checked to see whether it had been fired. It hadn't, and that was it."

"And that was here when you found him?" She pointed to a flashlight at the side of the terrace.

"Yes, it couldn't have been on. I would have found him a lot faster if I was homing in on a light."

Sue pulled on some latex gloves and carefully picked up the flashlight. After examining it closely, she toggled the switch. "It's dead. Must have been on its way out when he started up here."

Ray watched her bag the light.

"Let me shoot some photos of this area, and then let's have a good look around. Then I need lunch."

Ray was working at the whiteboard when Sue arrived with lunch. She sorted out the contents of the brown paper bag.

"One kefir smoothie made with frozen blueberries, mangos, peaches, and strawberries. Five pieces of candied ginger and one half teaspoon of turmeric added before blending. And for dessert one small fair trade, organic, pesticide free, 94% dark chocolate bar."

"Perfect," said Ray, without turning around. "What are you having?"

"A bacon cheeseburger. The cheese is artisanal, sustainable, with no GMOs."

"Good. Is that all?"

"Of course not. Sweet potato fries and an extra chunky chocolate chip cookie. And a diet Coke."

"One day you are going to weigh more than 110 pounds."

"And when I do, I'll start eating like you."

Ray continued writing. Finally, he settled at the table, and turned his attention to lunch.

"The only new piece of information is now we know why Gillian had hiking clothes in her car. A quick change and she would be ready to ride an ATV over to Ursidae," said Ray.

"If we accept Randy's story, if he had shown up she might not have been murdered. Which brings us to the question, how did someone know she was going to be there."

"How about this," said Ray, "her killer followed her from town. She gave him a perfect place for the attack, a deserted location. He might have been planning to attack her in the parking lot near her condo. On her way out here, Gillian probably didn't pay any attention to headlights behind her until she got to Pelkin Hill Road. Then she assumed they were Randy's. She probably assumed everything was going as planned until it was too late."

"So what are we left with?" said Sue.

"It all goes back to Phillip Lovell and Ursidae Winery. And we know, given the over-the-top tour Lovell gave me, whatever Gillian was looking for isn't there anymore." He consumed his smoothie, then turn his attention to the chocolate. "You want some of this?" he asked, holding half of the bar in her direction.

"Never turn down chocolate."

"Okay," said Ray, standing and going to the whiteboard, "this is what I've been working on." He motioned toward a list of names under Gillian Mouton.

Phillip Lovell
Gregory Mouton
Sherry Mouton
Blythe Erickson
Geoffrey Fairfield
Randy Donaldson

Did I miss anyone?"

"No. That's it as far as we know."

"And we've talked to all of them," said Ray. "Is there anyone we need to interview again?"

"We need to talk to Lovell again, but not until we have something more substantial."

Ray moved to the next column. "And I've done the same thing for Gregory Mouton. We know that Geoffrey Fairfield knew Gillian and also Gregory Mouton's father. We don't know if he and Gregory were acquainted."

"How about Fairfield and Sherry Mouton?"

"We have no evidence that they know each other, but it's certainly a possibility. Are you suggesting the possibility of a relationship?"

"She was younger and more vital than her husband. He didn't seem to be aging well."

Ray shook his head. "Mouton and his wife seemed to be happily married. I don't see her with Fairfield. I think he'd go for something a bit flashier."

"Like Gillian?"

"Exactly."

"How about suicide?" asked Sue. "Mouton could have figured out how to rig the explosion."

"Yes, but why. No suggestion that he was depressed or suicidal."

"We didn't ask," said Sue.

"Don't you think it would have come up?"

"People don't like to talk about mental illness. Sherry Mouton seems to play things close to the chest. Even if she suspected the possibility...."

"Yes," agreed Ray. "Leave the dead alone."

"You mentioned earlier the possibility that Gillian might have shared some important information with her stepbrother. Her killer then murdered him to make sure that stuff would go away forever."

"Then do they kill Sherry Mouton," asked Ray, "just in case her husband shared something with her? And if Gillian did tell her stepbrother something that led to her death, wouldn't he have told us?"

"They didn't have the best of relationships, Ray. Maybe he didn't care."

Ray took a marker and added bubbles near Sherry Mouton's name:

- Warn her to be extra cautious and explain why.

- Ask about depression.

- Ask if Gregory shared any suspicions as to why Gillian was murdered.

- Ask if Gregory knew Geoffrey Fairfield and if she knows him.

"Sue, we need to learn more about Gillian. Are you up to the New York trip? It should probably take a few days."

"We're in the same place. I had been thinking about that almost from the beginning of the investigation. From the beginning we've been stalled because we don't know much about Gillian's life. That problem hasn't changed. I keep wondering why was she here in the first place? We know the ostensible reason, her food and wine event, but was that just a cover? I'd like to talk to her lawyer, her accountant, people connected with her online site, and perhaps have a look at her apartment."

"How much bureaucracy are you going to have to cut through?"

"Not much, I've already got a contact in the prosecutor's office. I just need proper identification and a death certificate for Gillian."

"When could you go?" asked Ray.

"Tomorrow morning or Monday if I can get flights and have things arranged in New York. I should probably be able to accomplish everything in two workdays and be back by Tuesday or Wednesday. As soon as we are done here, I'll start working on getting to New York. You'll look after Simone?"

"Of course, she's always a joy. I've really become attached to her."

"Me, too," said Sue. "If either of us ever moves away, we'll probably end up in a bitter custody battle."

"There's one more thing," said Ray, "the destruction of the plants at Terroir Nord. That's not random vandalism. So who is the target, Marty? I think not. The boys? At this point I'd put my money on Randy—some husband or boyfriend getting a bit of revenge?"

"Come on, Ray, time to jump into the twenty-first century. We can handle a chainsaw with the best of them. Maybe it's a woman sending Randy a message that she's cutting him out of her life. She's probably a poetic type who prefers the symbolic cutting of vines to taking a saw to Randy's limbs. "

Ray sat silently, contemplating how to respond.

"You're seldom without a retort," she chortled.

"I was thinking about an opera or a country and western song with lyrics about chainsaws, love, root cutting, and revenge."

"You've got the makings of a singer-songwriter, Elkins."

"Yeah, I just need a twangy voice."

"So, if I go to New York, what are you going to do?"

"I'll talk to Sherry Mouton again. I'll call her before I leave the office. I'll try to see her as soon as possible. I'll tell her she might also be in danger, and I'll find a way to raise the possible suicide issue. See if our conversation leads anywhere else. I'll check on Randy Donaldson's alibi. And maybe I can have a conversation with Marty Donaldson if the doctors let me."

37

Ray was napping on a couch—Simone on his chest, also asleep—when Hanna Jeffers pushed her way into the door holding a large foam cooler in her arms.

Ray opened an eye in her direction.

"Don't you ever lock your doors?" she asked, dropping the container on the center island. "Looks like the two of you have had a hard day."

"Yes, the first bad thing about it was that it started in the middle of the night. If you hadn't dropped in, we might have slept through till morning."

"Well, forget that. The hunter-gatherer is here with a very special surprise. You and your woman friend better start waking up. I'll have dinner on the table in half an hour or less. Why don't you take Simone for a walk and tie your boat on my car while I get dinner on the table."

"What's the menu?"

"Special surprise."

"I'm not sure I have enough energy to...."

"Come on, Ray. Buck up. We'll just do a fast paddle, an hour or less. You'll feel better and sleep better after. Trust me, I'm a doctor."

When Ray returned to the kitchen twenty minutes later, candles were burning on the dinner table and the house was filled with wonderful aromas.

"Sit down and close your eyes, no peeking," Hanna ordered.

Ray followed her instructions, finally opening his eyes when commanded.

"One of my colleagues was in Ann Arbor for a few days," Hanna explained. "I had him bring back all the fixings for a Zingerman's Pastrami Brooklyn Reuben. Everything is fresh and perfect."

"Amazing. Thank you."

Ray carefully inspected the sandwich: the meat, the crusty pumpernickel, the Emmentaler Swiss, sauerkraut, and the Russian dressing. Before taking a bite, he lifted the sandwich and inhaled its bouquet. Then he carefully took a bite and chewed slowly, enjoying the complex mixture of flavors and textures.

"Don't dawdle over your food. There's not a lot of sunlight."

Ray looked across the table, momentarily taking her hand. "I'm not going to wolf this down. I'm going to linger long enough to savor every bite. And then I imagine there's a dessert?"

"Life is more than pastrami," she answered. "Two Magic Brownies. They almost disappeared as I was driving from town. It took all of my willpower not to pull to the side of the road and pillage through the container looking for the them. And that's why we have to go kayaking. Gotta burn those calories."

Thirty minutes later, they were rolling toward the big lake, Hanna at the wheel. Ray was slightly reclined in his seat, with Simone curled up in his lap. After the short drive, Hanna parked at a trailhead near the site of an old cannery, a launching point protected from southerly winds by Sleeping Bear Point. They carried their kayaks along a path through the dunes to the shore.

"Ventilation for Simone?" Hanna asked when they returned for their gear bags.

"It's cooling off. Just crack the windows a bit and leave the sunroof open an inch or two."

They paddled toward the setting sun, the quiet water mirroring the spectrum of muted twilight colors. As the bows of the kayaks cut through the water, elegant waves peeled away from the hulls. There was little conversation, just the sensual delight of moving across still water on a warm autumn evening.

"We should probably turn around," said Hanna, "if we want to make it back before it's completely dark."

"Hard to do," Ray answered. "There won't be many more evenings like this."

They turned and headed toward the shoreline, then paddled north, parallel with the beach. As they rounded the headland near their launch point, Hanna said, "Sounds like a car alarm."

As they approached the beach, she said, "Ray, that's my car."

They picked up the cadence. Ray propelled his kayak onto the beach, ripped off his spray skirt, and sprinted for the parking area. The driver's side door of Hanna's car was open; shards of glass covered the surrounding pavement. He checked the interior, and then scanned the area and surrounding dunes and shore. "Simone!" he shouted repeatedly, his eyes surveying the perimeter of the parking area and the nearby shore and woods.

"Oh, Ray," Hanna moved close, sliding under his arm. "What do we do now?" she asked.

"What did you leave in the car?" he asked.

"Nothing important," Hanna answered as she showed Ray a small dry bag she had carried in her boat. "Everything is in here: keys, wallet, phone."

"Let me use your phone and call dispatch. Mine's in the boat."

Hanna called out for Simone and quickly covered the paved area and adjoining land as Ray talked on the phone. Then he joined her in a frantic search as shadows grew longer and the light began to disappear on the horizon.

"If she were around, she would have come back by now," said Ray as they walked toward Hanna's damaged vehicle. "I hope she wasn't lured away by the coyotes. I don't believe this. This doesn't happen, especially at this time of year. We were targeted. Let's check the car again."

Ray opened all four doors and scanned the interior. "It doesn't look ransacked. Does anything look like it's been touched?"

"No. Are you going to call Sue?"

Ray leaned against the front fender and looked out at the dark water. "I don't think so. She's probably in bed by now. She's on the early flight. If I call her, she'll spend the whole night out here searching. I'll do everything that can possibly be done."

"Yes, but…."

"I know. I'll deal with the consequences." Ray inspected the car, circling once, then returning to the shattered window. "There's something wrong here. This doesn't fit. It wasn't a smash and grab. Other than Simone, there was nothing to take, no cameras or purses." He paused for a moment, and then asked, "Did you notice anyone following you? Either coming from town or as we headed out here?"

"No, but I probably wouldn't have unless they were hanging on my back bumper. I don't think I've ever thought about that possibility."

"Your car wouldn't be hard to pick out, especially with the kayaks. There are only a handful of us this late in the season, maybe three or four cars in the county, still carrying serious boats. Let's get our gear up here. There's a wrecker and a patrol car on the way."

"What about my car?"

"It's a crime scene. It's going to the county garage for the night. I'll have it processed tomorrow on the off chance there are fingerprints or other possible evidence. Then we'll get it to the dealership and get you a new window."

"And Simone?"

"We will reach out to the media and the network of organizations that help find lost pets."

"Are you okay?"

"No." Ray surveyed the area, hoping to see the small brindle terrier scamper his way. He felt his world was going out of control.

38

Ray had been up well before dawn and on the beach by first light searching for Simone. A few curious seagulls floated overhead on a gentle morning breeze, offering an occasional commentary on the frenzied human activity below. Eventually he gave up the search.

Standing in the parking lot, he called Sherry Mouton. Like the previous evening, there was no answer. He left a second message that he needed to speak with her. Later in the morning, after a third call, he decided to drive to her house.

Shorty after 10:00 he rolled up the long gravel drive to the old rambling farmhouse now solely occupied by Sherry Mouton. Her Saab was parked near the door. He ran his hand over the hood as he walked toward the door.

"Sheriff. I was just going to call you. I just got your messages. I had the phone turned off last night. Took a sleeping pill and I ended up oversleeping. I just made some coffee, would you like some?"

"That would be wonderful," he said, settling down on one of the antique spindle wood chairs that surrounded the old oak table.

"Milk, sugar, cream?" she asked as she slid a steaming mug of coffee in front of him.

"No, this is perfect. Thank you. I asked you before, but I'd like to go over this again. We're trying to find a motive for Gillian's murder. She spent several hours with your husband during her visit. I wonder what they talked about and whether he shared anything with you later?"

"No, nothing. Exactly what I told you before. I didn't like the woman. I was sort of ticked that he wasted so much time on her."

"Now if your husband was killed because of his connection to Gillian, you might be in danger, too."

"Do you really think so?"

"It's a possibility. I should have mentioned it earlier. Maybe you should consider staying with your neighbors or some other friends for the near future as we continue our investigations. And leave your car behind, it would be an easy way to track you."

"My neighbors have already suggested that I stay with them. I'll probably do that.

"Sheriff, I made some pie yesterday with apples from our little orchard. Would you like a piece to go with your coffee?"

Ray hesitated for a moment before answering. "If it's no trouble, yes. I skipped breakfast."

After the pie, more coffee, and some small talk, Ray asked, "Gregory, did he ever struggle with depression?"

Sherry picked up the coffee pot and topped off Ray's mug. "Well, I don't think Gregory was a depressive. It's not like he had spent years going to psychiatrists. He was a pretty happy person when I met him. That was one of his attractions, always smiling and joking. But the last few years had been difficult.

"Gregory was used to having a lot of money, not that we were rich. We were comfortable. We traveled, went to Florida in the winter every year for a few weeks, skied in Colorado. We even went to Hawaii for one of our anniversaries. We had a nice house and newish cars.

"That was the life Gregory had always known. It was his norm. And for me, the way the Moutons lived, that was pretty foreign to my growing up. My dad worked on the line at Dodge. My folks always lived from one paycheck to the next. There was always a lot of tension about money. So when Gregory and I first got together, I was amazed. Money, it was a non-issue for them. There was always enough, and there seemed to be an unending supply.

"When our business started to falter…Gregory really struggled, Sheriff. And I don't know how to explain it. I think part of it is that whole masculine thing. Like I know how hard it was for him to give up his membership in the Birmingham Country Club. It meant nothing to me, I never quite fit with those people, but it was a big deal for Gregory, a loss of face.

"And after that, it was just one thing after another. We cut back as much as we could. In the good days, we went from work to a nice restaurant. When things were falling apart, we went home, and I made dinner. I didn't mind. We were eating more healthily, and he was drinking less.

"But yes, he was down. His internist gave him some pills. Gregory called them his *happy pills*. But they didn't make him any happier. The life that he knew and loved was going away, and he never got used to that. I thought when we got up here permanently things would be better. Gregory would be away from that old environment. Sadly, that didn't happen. And after his father died, he became even gloomier."

"Did he continue taking antidepressants?"

"Well, I was hoping he was weaning himself off of them. He told me he was, but I don't think that was the case."

"And alcohol?"

"That continued to be a problem. Downstate his drinking was all part of being social, something he did in the evening when relaxing with friends. And I used to drink with him. It was part of our life together. After we moved north it changed. I stopped. I didn't need it anymore. Gregory kept drinking. Midmorning he'd have his first beer, and he'd keep drinking most of the day. Not that he was ever really drunk. Like I don't think he was ever a real danger on the road. He got that big belly, something he'd never had before. I tried to talk about it, but he wasn't interested in that conversation. He told me to leave him alone. It wasn't my concern."

"Where there other changes in his behavior?"

"He started gambling after his dad died, something he hadn't done much during the course of our marriage. He'd disappear, and then I wouldn't see him again for hours. He needed something to do, a job. I tried to get him to look for work, but he wouldn't hear about it. Said no one would give him a decent job at his age. It was that whole pride thing. If he couldn't be the boss, he didn't want the job. And when I told him I was looking for a job...."

Ray watched her wipe away tears with a sleeve and then grab a box of tissues. "We were starting to argue. It reminded me of my parents. It was something I had always hated."

"Was the marriage coming apart?"

"I don't think so. It was a rough time, but I believed we would get through it. But now with everything...I just don't know. I hate to think it might be true, that I would miss the warning signs. But maybe what happened was Gregory's way of dealing with things." She paused and looked away, over Ray's shoulder through the windows overlooking the woods beyond. "I think I was blind to what was going on. Maybe I wasn't there for him when he needed me the most."

Ray stood, "When I arrived I noticed the hood on your car was warm. You told me you overslept."

"I did, I really did. After I made coffee I found the cream had gone sour. You know how it rises and floats on the surface. I ran down to the village for some cream."

As Ray drove down the steep drive, he was wondering what part of her story he should believe. A few miles down the road he pulled off the road at a small access point and parked facing the water. He checked the time, and then dialed Sue's number. In a few seconds she was on the line.

39

Before driving back to County Center, Ray made a side trip and returned again to the parking area near the cannery, getting out, and calling for Simone. He closed his eyes for a few seconds and imagined her running toward him, followed by her usual reception, the joyful bark, the wagging tail, and the flurry of wet kisses. But no such sight greeted him as he opened his eyes, only sand, water, and the surrounding woods. He did a quick circuit of the area and then returned to his vehicle. As he slowly drove out of the parking area, he noticed a lost dog poster stapled to an electrical pole. Bringing the car to a stop, he climbed out and inspected the poster. Below the photo of a cairn terrier was a concisely written paragraph with all the relevant data. At the end was the non-emergency number for Cedar County Central Dispatch.

"How did you get the posters up so quickly?" Ray asked Jan as he walked into the office.

"I got started on it as soon as I read your email this morning. Followed our usual protocol for lost pets and sent emails to all the animal welfare groups in the area and the animal control officers in the region. I also contacted the radio stations that still do this type of local content. Now that my husband is retired, he needs things to do. Putting up the posters was a perfect job for him."

"Where did you get the photo?"

"Pulled it off the Web. Dog doesn't have the personality of Simone, but it pretty much looks the same."

"And you talked to Sue?" asked Ray.

"She called right after you talked to her. She assumed I'd be organizing the search. I could tell she was very concerned."

"Any response?"

"Nothing yet, Ray. These things sometime take days or weeks. And if the coyotes…."

"Don't even go there."

Jan moved to Ray's office door and quietly closed it. "Just to be on the safe side," she said nodding toward the door. "County Commissioner Melvin Feilen stopped in first thing this morning. He was demanding an immediate audience. He wanted to know where you were, why you weren't here, and when you were going to be available."

"My day is not getting any better."

"He wants to know what happened to Marty Donaldson, and he was sputtering on about how the farmers might have to form vigilante patrols because they're not getting any protection from 'overpaid and incompetent public employees who spend most of their time joyriding around on the county's dime.'"

"Where is Feilen now? I'd like to get this over with."

"He's in some subcommittee meeting. I've been instructed to make sure that you're available to have a conversation with him when he's finished. He's such an officious little weasel."

"If I'm here when he comes back, I'll talk to him."

Twenty minutes later, Ray was answering emails when Jan guided Feilen into his office.

"You're a hard man to find, Elkins," he said, settling into a chair directly across the conference table from where Ray was working.

"I'm here every day, sir. And if I happen to be away from the office, my staff always knows where I am."

"Well, good for them. I need to know about Marty Donaldson. I understand he was badly beaten and left to die in one of his vineyards the other night. By all reports it took your office more than an hour to respond."

"What's the source of your information?"

"Why do you ask?"

"Marty Donaldson was found in his vineyard unconscious. There was no evidence that he had been beaten. He has a long history of heart trouble, and it appears that he has had a major cardiac incident. I personally responded to the 911 call, our other two responders were both tied up. From the time I climbed out of bed until I was at his side was less than 20 minutes."

"Well, someone was killed in that same vineyard, right?"

"Correct, a week and a half ago. We've provided the media with daily briefings on that case. I'm sure you've seen reports on TV or in the papers."

"And why don't you have the killer? I imagine poor Marty was out there in the middle of the night just trying to protect his land. Things have really gone to hell in a handbasket when the citizens of Cedar County can't depend on local law enforcement to protect them or their property. I was just sharing my views with county board members. Let me tell you I'm not alone in my concern over your feckless leadership. And my phone has been ringing off the hook. People are afraid, Elkins."

Ray sat quietly, listening to the tirade, as he concentrated on his breathing. "Is there anything else, sir?" he asked, when Feilen briefly sputtered to a halt.

"Yes, there is, as a matter of fact. Last spring we had that cherry orchard vandalized. There have never been any arrests, let alone anyone being brought to trial. And this is just what I'm talking about. What do you and your people do all day? Why aren't you closing these cases?"

"In point of fact, sir, we close almost all of our cases. And the careful work performed by this department usually leads to successful prosecutions."

"Well, what about that orchard?"

"It's an open investigation...."

"Open my...."

"Is there anything else, sir? As you can see, I have a lot of work to attend to."

"Well you need to know —— and I'm trying to be your friend, Elkins — that people are upset with your job performance. They're remembering what a wonderful job old Sheriff Orville did over many decades when he ran the office. That man got things done. Orville understood law and order. He wasn't afraid to bust a few heads to get the bad guys in jail. He hired real men. He didn't have a bunch of pointy-headed deputies with college degrees running around the county looking at computer screens.

"And, Elkins, Orville understood the constitution and law enforcement. We weren't having any problems with illegals, voter fraud was unheard of, and no one was messing with our guns."

Ray stood. "Thank you, sir, for taking time to share your concerns. I really must get back to work."

"I'm just trying to help you out, Elkins. If you listen to me you might be able to avoid a disaster if you choose to run for reelection."

"I understand you're considering a run for the state senate yourself."

"People like my values. They know I have strong opinions. I tell it like it is. It's a winning model. You might want to emulate it, Elkins, especially if you want to keep your job," Feilen retorted as he stormed out.

Jan came in with a fresh flask of coffee. "How did it go?"

"The usual BS," said Ray.

"I don't know how you keep from exploding."

"Most days I can take his insane version of the world. Today he was pushing it."

40

The periodic TSA announcements were muffled by the sound of a riding vacuum making long passes in the airport's sparsely populated entry hall. A few people waited beyond the security entrance, some carrying small signs for local resorts or transportation companies. Ray checked the digital flight board again. The last flight from Detroit was listed as *delayed*. Then he checked a flight app on his phone. The plane, hours late, was on final approach to Traverse City.

He stood and waited as the tired passengers filed by, most dragging carry-ons. Sue was one of the last passengers down the connecting hallway. They embraced briefly, then started heading toward an exit, Ray now handling her carry-on as she shouldered a computer bag and small backpack.

"Sorry about the time."

"It was out of your control."

"The flight from New York was on schedule. Detroit was a nightmare. We were more than an hour late boarding, something about waiting for a crew that was on a delayed flight." They paused at a traffic crossing. "How are you? Tired, I bet. Anything new on Simone?"

"It's a complicated story," he answered as they walked to the parking area. "I'll tell you about it during the drive."

He popped the trunk, then stood and watched as Sue opened the door. Simone catapulted out of the car, circling and jumping, filling the air with joyful barking. Sue took the small dog into her arms and sobbed gently as she accepted a flurry of wet kisses.

Once they were settled in the car and were driving north, Sue said, "Why didn't you tell me, Ray?"

"This all came together about noon. Jan took a call from the St. Ignace Police Department. One of their officers found a collarless dog matching Simone's description in the central business area. Jan told them about the microchip and asked them to take the dog to a vet for identification.

"As soon as I heard it was Simone, I was heading for the Straits of Mackinac. I can't tell you how happy I was to have her in my arms. She insisted on being in my lap all the way back. Hard crossing the bridge with a dog who insists on kissing you every few minutes."

"St. Ignace, how did she get there?"

"That's the great mystery. I talked with the officer who found her. He said Simone was cold, wet, and didn't hesitate to jump into his patrol car when he opened the door to get out and check on her. He thought that was a bit unusual. It's been his experience that most dogs head the other way. When he got her back to the station, their dispatcher remembered seeing Jan's email alert. And then it all fell together. But to answer your question, someone had to drop her there. Simone didn't walk across the bridge."

"I don't understand," said Sue.

"The day Simone was snatched, we were followed to the beach. The dognapping was planned, not just a random or impulse event. And then someone went to a lot of trouble driving Simone all the way up to the U.P. The question is why?"

"Curious indeed. If they were trying to get back at you or Hanna for some reason, they would have probably killed her, left the body where you would have been sure to find it."

"Not a happy thought," said Ray.

"How about Hanna's car? Did you find anything?"

"Brett Carty carefully processed it. You've taught him well, by the way. He found my prints and Hanna's, no others. He did find a bit of fabric, little more than a few threads."

"And?"

"Brett showed them to me. Cotton, sort of the color and texture of a well-worn Carhartt jacket."

"That cuts our pool of suspects to about half the men in northern Michigan," said Sue. "An arrest on dognapping is imminent. What's happening with Marty Donaldson? Have you been able to interview him?"

"Yes, briefly. He's still a pretty sick guy. Marty remembers having trouble sleeping, having a dream about something more happening at that vineyard. He got up and drove there. He thought he saw something moving in the moonlight, and he walked up to have a look. Then he remembers feeling dizzy and sick and the world fading away."

"Gillian, what did you learn?"

"To begin with, superficial as it may be, I'm beginning to get a sense of who she was. Loved her apartment, tastefully done. I especially admired the furniture and the decorating. And the neighborhood, it's really cool. I'm not sure I'd want to live there, but it would be a great place to hang out occasionally. She had a closet full of lovely clothes. Everything was in perfect order awaiting her return. I didn't find a diary or anything else that would add to what we know. Her personal and business life all seemed to be on her computer and other devices. We've had those from the beginning."

"Any problem getting access?"

"None. A young assistant district attorney was assigned to assist me. He was terrific, drove me around and ran interference. Her lawyer was very cooperative, as was her financial manager. You will have a full report to peruse sometime tomorrow. I was working on it on the flights and during the layover. One of the interesting bits I picked up was that Gillian was always short of money. She was making a name for herself in a very competitive market. According to her finance guy, Gillian was always just a step or two ahead of a financial disaster. The cost of running a state-of-the-art website with video that changed daily required a website developer, videographers at different sites, a social media analyst, and a video producer. He said Gillian had recently told him that she was working on something that would bring in several million dollars and give her increased credibility in the industry."

"Did he know what that something was?"

"No, she wasn't giving away any of the details. He did say that Gillian was one of the most determined people he had ever met. He added that she could be totally ruthless and had probably made some enemies along the way."

41

Ray was still on the far edge of consciousness when his cellphone started to chime. Picking it up and entering the code, he looked at the small display: 4:26. *Never good news,* he muttered to himself.

"Sheriff, this is Central. Sorry to awaken you, but I thought you'd want to know. We have a major structure fire. Road patrol is on the scene. They made the initial call. Structure's fully engulfed. Fatalities possible. The fire company has requested assistance."

"Home? Business?"

"Residence, on the bay."

"Send me the address. I'm on the way."

A few minutes later, dressed in fleece warm-ups and a Cedar County Sheriff's Department nylon jacket, Ray slid into his patrol car. After starting the engine, he peered at his computer screen and copied the address into the GPS software. Once he was on the county's one major highway driving north, he played with the touch screen to get a sense of his final destination. Then he lifted the microphone of his radio and squeezed the transmit button.

"Central, please send me any owner information."

Occasionally he glanced over at the display. A new line appeared in the message box. *Fairfield, Geoffrey.*

From that point forward he didn't need the GPS, the glow from the blaze was being reflected back from the low hanging clouds. Nearing the scene, Ray pulled to the shoulder on a small rise a hundred yards back and viewed the conflagration below. The structure was at the end of a small finger-like peninsula that reached out into the bay. A long drive snaked in from the highway.

The dark figures of the firefighters were silhouetted against brilliant light as an explosion un-seamed the old frame structure. The walls of the first level collapsed and the second story dropped straight down and broke apart, releasing a shower of sparks into a hellish vortex that danced skyward.

Ray drove down to the entrance drive, parking just off the road, the flashing light bar on his vehicle's roof illuminating the pavement. An array of emergency vehicles was positioned on the drive and lawn, well back from the fire. The remains of the building continued to roar and hiss as the first columns of water from the high-pressure hoses slammed into the inferno.

As he started to walk in toward the fire, Ray noticed a black convertible sitting on a side drive next to the garage well back from the house. Ray looked at the letters on the vanity plate. RAVEN.

"It was over before we got here," explained Bernie Rathman, the township fire chief, over the clanging of the big diesel. "Gasoline, Ray, I could smell it, even with all the fire. The place was torched. Lots of accelerant, gallons."

"Anyone around, any sign of survivors?"

"Haven't seen anyone. Not even gawkers. Nearby houses must be seasonal."

Rathman moved away, providing direction to his crew. Ray tromped around the perimeter of the activity, skirting the hose used to pull water from the bay to the pumper. He climbed up on the rock seawall and watched as the crew slowly brought the flames under control and then focused on the remaining hotspots. An onshore breeze carried the stench of the fire away from him.

In the dull, predawn light, the faces of the people whom he had encountered during the investigation passed before him. First he saw Gillian, a crumbled corpse in the dew-covered vineyard. He thought about the vibrant Gillian, the woman on her website, but he couldn't hear her voice, or see her face clearly.

Ray's vision of Gregory Mouton was more complete. He could see the large man settling in a chair, sharing stories of Gillian and their last boat ride along the dunes. The sight, sound, and body language were all there. Then he remembered his last view of Mouton, his face distorted by the crushing force of an explosion.

Geoffrey Fairfield was more of a mystery. Ray thought back to their one encounter. Fairfield had finely honed social skills. His answers to their questions seemed to be measured, like Fairfield was carefully crafting his own history.

And then there was Sherry Mouton, the one person of the four with whom he had spent more time. Ray thought about how her story had changed in the course of their three interviews. Was she more open as she became comfortable with him, or was she finally able to admit her husband's depression to herself by talking to him? Or was this all a tale to cover a secret romance? How many bodies were they going to find in this house? He had wanted to believe her. He had difficulty seeing her involved in the death of her husband.

Ray turned and looked east toward the horizon. There was still no hint of the approaching dawn. He looked down at the dark water lapping against the seawall, its sound obscured by engines.

Wearily, he skirted the firefighters and their equipment as he made his way back to the highway. For the next few hours he helped one of his deputies control traffic. After they were relieved by members of the day shift, he returned home and stood in the shower for a long time, trying to wash away the stench of fire and destruction.

Later in the morning Ray returned with Sue to the Fairfield fire scene. The blue Suburban belonging to Mike Ogden, the state police arson investigator, was parked near the one remaining fire engine. A small crowd of firefighters was gathered near the back hatch of Ogden's truck, most holding paper coffee cups.

"Guess we better get back to work," joked Ogden, noting Ray's appearance. "Coffee?" he asked, holding out a stack of cups and a large thermos bottle.

"Sure," Ray answered, joining the group.

"Ray, I'm working on a possible scenario."

"Okay," Ray responded.

Ogden motioned toward Bernie Rathman. "Bernie was giving us his impressions when he first arrived on the scene."

"Flames were pouring out of the doors and windows. I didn't think much about it at the time. My focus was helping my crew get lines in place and water pumping."

"This is what's going on, Ray," said Ogden, leading the way to where the house once stood. "Look at the doors to the cellar. They were obviously open, slightly scorched, but showing very little damage. No one on your crew would have opened them?" Ogden asked, looking toward Rathman.

"No," he answered. "I didn't notice them at the time, but that's the way it must have been."

"Think about a perfectly constructed campfire," explained Ogden. "You layer the twigs, then sticks, and finally logs so air can be pulled in at the bottom and funneled up through the combustible material. Now think about this house. It's an old wooden structure, maybe a century or more. Bernie says there was a strong smell of gasoline when he first arrived. I'll test for that. But let's assume it's the case. An arsonist could provide a good draft at the base of the fire by opening these doors and any interior doors that would block the airflow. Opening doors and windows would further enhance the airflow and combustion.

"So back to Bernie. I know you've fought a lot of structure fires over the years. Was this different?"

"When we first got here flames were pouring out of the front door. It was open. And fire was pouring out of windows on the second floor. The thing with the windows seemed different. As the building heats, the glass breaks. But in this case the windows didn't seem to be in the way of the fire. Maybe someone had opened them, all of them. I wish I had some video to show you what I'm saying."

"One carefully constructed fire, worthy of a merit badge," said Ogden. "The gasoline splashed around the basement and first floor would quickly provide the heat to ignite the wood and other combustible materials in the structure. And once the dry old wood started to burn, you'd have the fuel for a very hot fire. Almost everything was incinerated."

"How about the victims?"

"At this point we believe there were two people in the structure," answered Rathman. "The remains were found in the basement area; we can only guess where they were when the fire started."

Ray looked over at Dyskin.

"The remains have been bagged. Both bodies were badly charred. Identification will have to be through dental records."

"Gender?" asked Ray.

"Like I said, both bodies were badly charred. I'm not sure what the pathologists will be able to determine. Since the bodies were partially cremated, I think it's safe to assume the victims were on one of the two upper floors at the onset of the blaze. They were partially cremated before they fell into the basement as the house collapsed. It's going to be difficult or impossible to separate out injuries that happened before the fire as opposed to those that resulted from the fire and the subsequent collapse of the building. Ray, I had the bodies removed to eliminate any biohazard. Ogden wants to comb through what's left."

"Understood," Ray answered, looking at Dyskin.

"Anything I should know?" asked Ogden, looking at Ray and Sue.

Ray pointed back up the drive toward the garage. "That black convertible, the Saab with the vanity plates. It belongs to Sherry Mouton, the wife of the man killed in the boat explosion, Gregory Mouton."

"And the owner of this house, a connection?" asked Ogden.

"It looks like they were involved romantically," answered Sue.

"A possible love triangle? Maybe a murder suicide?"

"All of the above," answered Sue. "This investigation started with the murder of Gregory's stepsister, Gillian. The bodies are piling up, and at this point we have more questions than answers."

42

"New whiteboard?" asked Sue as she set a brown paper bag containing lunch on the conference table. Simone followed behind, dragging a leash. She circled the table and jumped into Ray's lap.

"I've liberated it from the county commissioners' meeting room. I don't think it's ever been used. The commissioners, they are more into talk. They don't do much writing. And my need is greater than theirs at the moment. I'll return it before anyone misses it."

"How's Simone today?" he asked.

"Really needy. She had some part of her anatomy against me all night, and she was clearly unhappy that I left her in the Jeep when I was at the scene. That poor little kid has had more trauma in her life than anyone ever should."

"If she could only tell us who snatched her…Sue, someone is playing with us."

"Can we eat while things are hot? I got you a variation on the usual, a tofu cutlet in a balsamic peanut butter sauce on a whole wheat bun."

Ray toyed with the wrapped sandwich as he scanned the text on an iPad.

"When did you eat last?" asked Sue.

" I got a sandwich in St. Ignace after I picked up Simone."

"Did you share?"

"Actually, I got two. Chicken breasts, grilled not breaded. Simone ate one, only the meat, not the bun."

"McDonalds."

"What can I say, the sustainable organic food movement hasn't made much progress in the U.P. yet." Ray paused for a minute as he unwrapped his sandwich. "I was just reading the notes on your New York trip. You must have been up early this morning."

"Our mutual friend here wanted a walk before 7:00."

"What should I pay special attention to?"

"The fact that Gillian was always short of money. She was working hard to keep her little empire afloat. She wasn't in this area just to do an event. She was clearly searching for something."

"So we know she pulled off one exposé that apparently got her a lot of press and presumably helped her business. I think we have to assume she was hoping to do something like that again, and we know she was focused on Lovell."

"Should I look at the parent company, see if they've been involved in any questionable business practices?" Sue asked, carefully cutting her burger in half with a plastic knife.

"Yes, that would be a start. We also have to look at the possibility of someone within the organization doing a little freelancing. You know, people stealing from the company and setting up a side business. We see it all the time up here in mom and pop businesses, professional practices, and even some of the larger companies. The other thing is that we've only focused on Phillip Lovell. What if it's one of his employees?"

"Ray, he's the face of the winery. He's the reason why Gillian was here."

"But what if he's been taken in?"

"I don't think so," objected Sue. "Look at the security in that place. And I'm sure there are corporate watchdogs. Even if he were incompetent, someone else…."

Ray was out of his seat moving toward the blank whiteboard positioned at the far end of the conference table. "Let's switch gears for awhile and think about this morning's fire. I'm assuming the bodies are Sherry Mouton and Geoffrey Fairfield. There was no attempt by the perpetrator to make this look like anything other than an arson/murder."

"What happened to murder/suicide?"

"I don't think so. Do you?"

"I don't know. It looks like a love triangle. Gregory is killed in an explosion. At first glance it looks like an accident. Sherry's story slowly evolves, so it starts looking like a possible suicide. Then Sherry and Geoffrey Fairfield die in a house fire. Did Sherry, with or without help from Fairfield, do in her husband to pursue a relationship? Was she spurned by Fairfield? Was this a murder suicide? The storyline has all the elements of soap opera. But why the fire, Ray?"

"Exactly. If this were a simple murder/suicide, we'd have a weapon, fingerprints, body positions, corpses, and all the other bits and pieces of evidence. We'd be able to tell with fairly great certainty what had happened. We'd also be able to tell if the crime scene had been rigged. Here we're left with nothing. Only supposition.

"So we need to start by getting lots of search warrants," said Ray, starting a list on the blank whiteboard. We need to go through Sherry Mouton's house and see if we can find anything that links her and Fairfield. The phones, computers, the whole nine yards. Process her car, his, too. It must be in the garage. See if Fairfield's prints show up in her house or car. Maybe her prints are in his car. And I remember Sherry told me she was close with her neighbor. That's the house just south of hers. Maybe Sherry shared something. Then there's Fairfield's business…."

"Independent insurance agent. He operated out of his home. Lots of luck finding any records, at least at the scene," said Sue. "I didn't see any fireproof file cabinets in the rubble."

"We need to know more about him and the business. What companies did he represent? It's going to be a hard one, Sue. I'm not sure many of the companies will be willing to talk to us unless we're investigating a specific incident."

"I'll get started with the search warrants. I might be able to find a judge for signatures during the weekend. That said, the phone companies and some of the other people we need to contact have this curious habit of normal business hours, Monday through Friday."

"If you get to the search warrants, that's fine, or they can wait till Monday."

"There was one more thing I was thinking about on the plane."

"What's that?"

"The goat lady."

"What about her?"

"She probably knew Gillian better than anyone else in the area. They were doing an event together. Might there have been something more that we don't know about?"

"No, I don't think so. I can't see how she would fit into any of this."

"Ray, you have this tendency to be rather blind when it comes to attractive earth-mother type women. Remember being taken in by the lovely Elise in her hand-woven outfits, the queen of organic foods, tie-dye, and sustainability. Too bad she turned out to be a cold-blooded killer."

"Not the same, Sue."

"Someone who handcrafts chèvre made from the milk of goats probably named after French feminist poets. She would have no trouble taking you in."

"Think about it, Sue. Is Hanna anything like that?"

"No, not really. But she's a kayaker. In your worldview that trumps everything."

43

"A Sunday morning phone call, Ray. I'm almost afraid to ask," said Sue, sleep still in her voice.

"A call came through dispatch from the FBI. Two bodies, badly decomposed, were found on North Manitou Island on Friday. They sent in a forensic anthropologist yesterday via a Coast Guard helicopter. We've been invited to be part of an interagency team to observe the scene and the process. Two bodies eight miles offshore, I think we need to be represented. The boat is going to depart this morning at 10:00."

"Ray, can you hear the wind? Have you noticed the rain? It's a howling storm out there. You know how seasick I get. Are you requesting or commanding?"

"Only a request. I thought you'd be interested in seeing the anthropologist work the scene."

"Yes, I would love that, but not in these conditions. You're the waterman, you go. We'll catch up tomorrow."

Dressed in a waterproof poncho and rain pants, Ray stood in the harbor and looked out across the lake. The surface was covered with whitecaps, some breaking over the seawall at the mouth of the harbor. He was one of the last to board.

The National Park Service boat started to bounce as soon as it cleared the protection of the harbor and turned into the face of the storm. The waves—propelled by gale-force winds and building over the 250-mile fetch on their northerly journey from somewhere south of Chicago—intensified as they were funneled between the Manitou Islands and the northeastern shore of Lake Michigan.

Ray huddled below deck with most of the other passengers for a few minutes. Feeling both claustrophobic and queasy, he worked his way toward the stern and out through the door onto the rear deck. Then, his hands tightly gripping the wet rungs, he cautiously climbed the ladder to the upper deck, stopping and bracing against the safety cage that surrounded the ladder as the boat pitched from side to side. Using the railings, his feet widely spaced for balance, he fought his way to the foremost part overlooking the bow, pulling himself next to the only other person on the upper deck.

"Just look at the horizon," the woman shouted at him over the cacophony of wind, waves, and a pounding diesel engine. "It will help."

Ray peered over at a rain-gear clad figure, only a bit of her face visible behind the tightly cinched hood. He followed her advice, focusing on the horizon, a dull gray line that gently curved against the darker gray of the water's jagged plane. He widened his stance, relaxed, and started to absorb some of the motion rather than fighting it.

The captain held a westerly course straight into the tall waves, the ship punching through the swells, some breaking over the bow, crashing into the slanted windows of the pilot house, and then sweeping up across the upper deck. Ray held tight as the spray smashed into his body. A respite of smaller swells would be followed by two or three tall waves, the foam blowing off their crests.

The captain turned south and slowed the engine. The ship rolled from side to side in the deep troughs of the waves. Finally, an ancient lake steamer—black with patches of rust—careened past them on a southerly course toward open water. Then the captain increased the throttle, turning the ship back on course.

The waves began to drop as they moved into the lee of the island. Ray felt his anxiety start to drain away as the ship finally moved behind the steel seawall. He started to slacken his grip on the railing. As the crew was securing the ship against the dock, Ray said to his companion, "National Park Service?"

"FBI," came her reply.

"Where did you acquire your sea legs?"

"Annapolis, followed by four years on Ticonderoga-class cruisers." She loosened and pushed back her hood. "And you. What's your...."

"Local Sheriff, Ray Elkins." He extended his right hand, his left still gripping the railing.

"So they want you in the loop. Cooperating agency," she held his hand briefly without giving her name.

"And you are?"

"Special Agent Irene Iznaola. They wanted me to see a forensic anthropologist work a scene as part of my training."

"Where did you start...?"

"D.C. Pulled off the tennis court yesterday afternoon. Told I would need hiking clothes, rain gear, possibly a sleeping bag, and the location and time the boat would be leaving the dock. No one mentioned the gale warnings." She smiled for the first time. "So it was just a quick hop to T.C. via Reagan, Atlanta, Minneapolis, a double miles deal. On the ground at midnight."

Other than the crew, they were the last ones off the boat, straggling behind the main group to the end of a long pier and then along a sandy path to a white clapboard building. Once the entire group was inside the building, a man in a National Park Service uniform handed out sandwiches and coffee over a cacophony of voices.

A few minutes later a tall, thin man in mufti cleared his throat, then made eye contact with the members of the small group. "I've met most of you over the years. I'm Adam Winneger, FBI-SAC. Sorry about the rough crossing. You all deserve a day of hazardous duty pay.

"I'm going to pass this off immediately to Bob Parker from NPS, the National Park Service. He's the chief ranger on the island. He'll brief you on what we know so far and what we hope to accomplish today."

"Welcome, everyone. My apologies, too, for the lumpy water. Normally we don't run the boats in weather like this. On the bright side, the sandwiches came over on the boat. They're fresh and the coffee is hot. And the cookies are worth the calories. Some of you might not be too interested in food for a few hours. Throw the sandwiches in your backpacks. You will want them later. We got a lot of cold wet miles ahead of us.

"Here is the background. Friday we had two campers, late season visitors, report finding some bones in a clearing on the west side of Manitou Lake." He pointed to a map taped to the wall behind him. "They were canoeing around the island, got caught in a squall, and came ashore and walked into the woods looking for cover. One of the individuals is in her last year in veterinary medicine at Michigan State. They stumbled onto the bones, and she started examining remains, thinking they were probably deer. It quickly became apparent what they had found. She and her companion hiked across the island and contacted us. One of our rangers, Ed Upton, accompanied them back to the scene. He verified their find. And the young vet, on further examination, affirmed again her belief that they were human remains. Let me pass this back to Agent Winneger."

"Based on their observations and extensive photos taken at the scene by the veterinarian and the ranger, the Bureau sent in a forensic anthropology team. This is something new for us. We've only been doing this for about three years. We found this approach to be invaluable in cases where there is little left but skeletal remains.

"The team arrived yesterday, fortunately under quite ideal weather conditions, and was able to get started on the scene. Our contact with your agencies—and let me apologize for the short notice—was the result of some of the early findings." He paused and scanned the group. "First, they found two bodies, not one as we had originally thought. Second, although the remains are in a high state of decay, the team thinks that they are relatively fresh, possibly four to six weeks old. The environment where the bodies were dumped and the warm temperatures this summer and fall contributed to rapid deterioration. There was no identification at the scene. Hopefully, we might find some clues in the bones that will help us with the cause of death.

"This is a very remote burial site in an isolated corner of the world. But the bodies didn't drop out of the sky. I think I can safely say that we're looking at a crime scene. Getting to the bottom of this will require a multiagency, multijurisdictional effort.

"We have to hike in to the scene, it's more than three miles each way, and that's as the crow flies. Lots of twists and turns through hilly terrain. And we're limited by available light. Before we begin, the facilities are just across the walk. One more thing, the boat may not be crossing back to the mainland today, the storm seems to be building. Ranger Parker assures me we will be provided food, sleeping bags, and a roof over our heads if that turns out to be the case."

"Your cell phones," interrupted Parker, "they only work on this side of the island. And then only intermittently, if at all. I'll be leading the hike to the scene. We will form up just outside in about 10 minutes."

44

S ue looked out of the kitchen window of the house next door to the Mouton property. She could hear the rattle of coffee cups behind her.

"I'm in shock," said Mary Tomlinson as she placed a cup and saucer in front of Sue. "You're sure it's Sherry? From what I heard on the news there wasn't anything left?"

"The identification was based on dental records."

Mary set a small tray on the table holding a sugar bowl and a cream pitcher.

"How well did you know Sherry Mouton?"

"We were friends, pretty close neighborly friends if you know what I mean. We're about fifteen years older than…well, they were. So we're sort of from different generations. I can't believe they're both gone. Just like that."

"Am I right in assuming that you had a relationship with them over the years?"

"Yes, we do go back a ways. We bought this place years ago. It started as a summer home, but we'd always planned to retire here. So we knew Mike, Greg's father, as well as the kids."

"How well did you know Sherry?"

"Like I said, neighbors. We weren't close like some women become. That said, in the last year we became much closer."

"Why was that?"

"It started last December when Dennis had a major heart problem. Between the initial diagnosis, the surgery, and some post-op complications, Dennis was in the hospital for more than three weeks. I'm really frightened of winter driving. The Moutons knew that and became my personal taxi service, especially Sherry. We spent lots of time together in the car and at the hospital. I don't know what I would have done without her." She left the table to get some tissue.

"It was during that time she started opening up to me," Mary continued. "She told me about their problems, Greg's drinking and gambling. I don't think he hit her or anything, but he wasn't being very nice to her and hadn't been for a while. And I could see it was wearing on her. Back in the day, they had seemed so happy." She added some cream to her coffee and slowly swirled it with a silver spoon. "Of course, that was before they lost the business and all. When they moved up here they had to change their lifestyle. Sherry seemed okay with it, but not Gregory. You could see the change. He was gone more than home. I think he was usually at the casino."

A long silence followed as the two women gazed on the Mouton farmstead surrounded by brilliant crimson maples.

"Beautiful place down there," observed Mary. "Hard to… understand. I don't know what I wanted to say."

"Did Sherry ever mention a Geoffrey Fairfield?"

"The fire, that was at his place?"

"Correct."

Mary looked at the ceiling, then back over at Sue. "I feel like I'm breaking a trust."

"Mrs. Tomlinson, we're trying to determine what happened. This is a murder investigation. Anything you can tell me will help us get justice for Sherry."

"There's a history here. What's the term everyone's using these days, the backstory. Sometime last fall, almost a year ago, Dennis and I were having dinner in Petoskey. It was our anniversary. I saw Sherry on the other side of the restaurant. She and a man were sitting close together, you know, in an intimate way. I was sort of startled when I noticed it wasn't Gregory. The man was younger than Gregory, smaller frame, and he had a full head of hair. I don't think she saw me until we were on our way out. They were seated

45

Ray found Sue working at the conference table in his office when he returned late Monday afternoon.

"How was the crossing?" she asked. "You look a bit green."

"Beam wind all the way. Lots of rock and rolling."

"I only got bits and pieces of your phone message," said Sue. "You were breaking up."

"I wanted to tell you about the bodies."

"Have you had lunch?"

"No."

"How about some coffee? I've got some Clif bars."

"Yes to both."

While she was gone, Ray started to outline the findings on the right side of the mostly blank whiteboard.

"Okay, start at the beginning, Ray. All I know is you said some human remains were discovered."

"And that's all I knew until we actually got to the site...."

"Which was?"

"On the west side of the island, near the shore. Have you been out there?"

"Never. Just a day trip to South Manitou once."

"The NPS has their headquarters on the east side where there's a protected dock area. There are also a few remaining buildings of an old village and summer colony. The bodies were discovered on the other side of the island. A chance find by a couple of campers."

"You said something about a forensic anthropologist. What are we talking about? Native American remains?"

"Hardly. That said, there wasn't much more than bones and clothing. The bacteria, insects, birds, and animals had all done their work. The bodies had been covered with brush, and perhaps a bit of soil had been tossed over the top. You could hardly call it a grave. Whoever dumped the bodies wasn't into heavy lifting. They probably didn't think the remains would ever be found, at least not anytime soon."

"I'm still in the dark, Ray."

"Two bodies, probably male. Best estimate is four to six weeks. By the time we hiked across the island the forensic anthropologist, a Dr. Breanna Ensign, had pretty much completed her initial survey of the site and then explained the process to us. I learned more over dinner."

"Any identification, cause of death?"

"No identification. There were some jeans and underwear, but no shoes or shirts. The skeletons were small, but mature. Ensign based that assessment on calcification in some of the bones and the condition of the teeth. Her best guess was that the remains were male, between 5'3" to 5'5" in height, and about thirty years of age. Based on the shapes of the skulls, she speculated that they were originally from Mexico or Central or South America. She said she would know more after the DNA analysis."

"Cause of death?"

"That was one area where there wasn't much speculation. The damage to the skulls suggests that both men had been shot from the rear, execution style."

"Bullets?"

"Not while I was there. It's a swampy area. They're going to have to do a lot of work screening soil. But I think the bullets will be found."

"Possible scenario? Where did they come from? How did they get there?" Sue questioned.

"That's the intriguing part. That western side of the island is mostly deserted, even during the tourist season. There are footpaths and hiking trails that crisscross the island and run along the perimeter, but that particular stretch of beach is especially isolated.

"Where did they come from? Might have been Wisconsin or almost anywhere on Lake Michigan or Huron, but most likely, somewhere close, probably from a nearby coastal area," Ray paused for a minute.

"You're thinking Cedar County, aren't you?" Sue asked.

"Not exactly. But I believe the perp was working in familiar territory. He knew where he could dispose of those bodies fairly easily. And to answer your last question – how did they get there – by boat, maybe a cruiser of some sort, then a skiff or Zodiac to the beach. Or maybe one of the larger Zodiac-type boats where they can run them right onto the beach. After that I don't know what to tell you. Who these people were or why they needed killing, that's the real mystery."

"Anything else?"

"I'm sure there will be more once she gets the remains back to her laboratory, but there were two things. First, the jeans. The labels had been cut out of them, but she said they looked similar to the ones sold by Walmart. Second, the left hand of one of the victims, the three middle fingers, the bones had been cut. Ensign said these were old injuries, consistent with occupational accidents in the packinghouses or construction. I think she was talking about carpenters and saws in the latter case." Ray paused and sipped some coffee. "I don't remember any recent missing persons report, either from our resident or migratory Hispanic population."

Sue opened her laptop, then her fingers raced across the keyboard. A few moments later she looked up. "Nothing here or in the region for several years. We could reach out to Father Sanchez, I know he works closely with the migrant community."

"That's a starting point."

"So Ray, unpack the story a bit. Tell me about the people, the terrain, where did you sleep, what did you eat, do you have pictures, video?"

"It was a small group, three rangers, a couple more FBI agents, and someone from the Michigan State Police – a young guy from Lansing I've never seen before. We had to hike to the scene on the other side of the island. The trail snakes across the island, lots of hills and valleys. It's mostly through dense forest. You're under this canopy of tall trees. There's nothing around here on the mainland that compares to that forest."

"I'm surprised they didn't drive you over."

"Once you get out of the old settlement area near the dock, there are no roads. The NPS has a couple of ATVs, but they were being used by the anthropology team to haul their gear. Sue, after that rough crossing, I liked the walk. I started to feel human again. After the last two weeks we've had, walking in the rain under the heavy forest canopy…it was peaceful, cleansing. It was a brief respite from the carnage. I just hung out at the end of the pack. I had a chance to talk with Irene Iznaola and find out a bit about her work. She's part of a team investigating human trafficking. The Bureau is looking at cases where people are smuggled into this country as a form of cheap labor. And this is the kind of thing we don't want to believe happens in the U.S. It might be women from Eastern Europe or Asia who are promised real jobs and end up being forced into prostitution. Or illegals from all over the globe, but especially Mexico and the southern hemisphere, who work in sweat-shops, farms, and slaughterhouses. They are subject to all kinds of abuse, routinely cheated out of their meager wages, and often disposed of when they have outlived their usefulness. And when I say disposed of, it's exactly that. Landfills, dumpsters, who knows what else. And if the bodies are ever found, local law enforcement seldom is even able to identify the victims. Since these people have no community or family missing them, there are seldom any investigations, let alone arrests or successful prosecutions. These are throwaway people, disposables."

"All this came out of a conversation walking up a path?"

"The hike out, the hike back, and over dinner with her, Dr. Ensign, and the others."

"Where was dinner?"

"The NPS usually puts up campers and hikers trapped on the island during bad weather in a pole building. We got lucky. A volunteer group working on the island this summer completed the restoration of an old Victorian boarding house, a summer resort kind of place. We were the first residents. They had sleeping bags and cots for us. There was a woodstove in the main room to take off the chill. The facilities were out back."

"And food?"

"The rangers were very inventive. They are in the process of mothballing the island for the winter. But they came up with the ingredients for chili and cornbread. The food was prepared using a period cookstove. We were all so cold and wet. It was perfect. At the end there was apple pie from trees that were planted by the early settlers. I saw the apples, very small and tart. It was a different taste. There was also some beer and wine, and a bottle of brandy at the end. The brandy was passed around, no glasses, some serious conversation before we crawled into our sleeping bags."

"The anthropologist?"

"Dr. Breanna Ensign, interesting person. She's an M.D., a pathologist. She'd had some undergraduate work in anthropology, actually took part in digs during her college years. Once she got into forensic pathology she was frustrated by the lack of…what should I say…techniques, science to deal with old crime scenes and badly deteriorated corpses. She went back and added a Ph.D. in anthropology. The woman is passionate, it's all about science, it's all about justice."

"So what were your takeaways?"

"There are amazing people in this country, people who dedicate their lives to protecting others. In spite of the grim findings, there was a sense of optimism. We were all part of an important mission. We were going to try to get justice for these men."

"Are the feds going to have a press conference…?"

"Yes," Ray looked at his watch. "At 5:00 at the NPS headquarters. They are trying to get on the evening news cycle and perhaps find some viewers with helpful information."

Ray pushed himself out of his chair and stretched. "Anything on the bodies in the fire?"

"I received dental records this morning. Let me check if there's anything new."

Ray moved behind her so he could read her screen.

"It's here," she answered, opening a PDF. A minute or two of silence followed before Sue uttered, "Oh my god! They were shot through the head, execution style."

46

Kristal Glenn, the Cedar County Building Inspector, stood next to her car at the side of the narrow gravel road. Ray pulled up behind her.

"What's going on?" he asked, walking to her side.

"I had barely gotten to my desk this morning when I got a call from one of the neighbors down the road," she pointed in an easterly direction, "that Feilen was at it again. He was knocking down a building with an end loader. I knew he hadn't pulled a demolition permit, so I drove out to serve him with a cease and desist order. I didn't think there would be any problem. We've known each other since the third grade. Not that we were buddies, but we've always been on speaking terms.

"So I rolled in there," she motioned toward the cement entry drive that ran into the old fruit processing complex, a collection of cement block buildings scattered across a field of cracked concrete and gravel. "After he climbed off the end loader, I said something like 'Melvin, you know you can't do that without pulling a permit.' I passed him the desist order, and the jerk grabbed it out of my hand and tore it up. A long stream of profanity followed, and he ordered me off his property. So I pulled my car out here and called dispatch."

"Did he threaten you physically?"

"Verbal abuse—bitch, government whore. He didn't touch me, nothing like that."

"Let's try to talk to him again," Ray said. "I'll alert dispatch and ask to have a couple of officers staged nearby if I need some help. My guess is that Feilen is just being stupid or pulling some kind of political stunt. Let's see if we can get this resolved without providing any photo ops or YouTube footage. Is he alone?"

"No, that weirdo that's hung with him for years is in there at the wheel of a dump truck. Know who I'm talking about? In high school we called him Doc Tenny because he looked so unhealthy. Rumor back then was he lived on beer, cigarettes, and Twinkies. I can't even remember his real first name."

"Al, Al Tenny," said Ray. "He's known to us. Occasionally boards with us at the Heartbreak Hotel."

"How does he keep a driver's license?"

"I don't think he's ever had one. Give me a few," said Ray as he walked back to his car.

Several minutes later Ray and Kristal Glenn walked across the wide expanse of deteriorating concrete to Melvin Feilen. He continued to ram the end loader into the remnants of an old block building, scooping up the mangled debris, and dumping it into the waiting truck. If Feilen saw them approaching, he did his best to hide it. Finally, Ray shouted at him.

Feilen glanced his direction, put the machine in idle, slowly dropped his long frame off the side, and walked in their direction.

"What can I help you with, Sheriff?"

"Sir, we've had complaints from citizens that you are not following the county building code. And Ms. Glenn says you've not filed for a permit to demolish a building. She's told me when she tried to serve you with a cease and desist order, you tore it up and ordered her off your property. Is that true?"

"It's all about castle doctrine, Sheriff. I'm protected by the castle doctrine law."

"Sir, Ms. Glenn is hardly an intruder. She's a representative of the government of Cedar County, and is clearly identified as such by her picture ID. She was here to ask you to stop tearing down that building until you've completed the necessary paperwork. This is not a home invasion in the dead of night. The castle doctrine doesn't apply."

"I beg to differ, Sheriff. The issue here is a broader interpretation of the castle doctrine. Why should government have anything to say about what I do on my own property? Why can't I tear down an old building? I mean, whose business is that other than my own? And why should I have to pay a fee so some bureaucrat can joyride around the county and put her nose where it's not needed. If you want to arrest me, go ahead. I'm sure it will get me lots of votes and lots of new donors."

"Mr. Feilen, this is my expectation. First, you'll turn off that machine and do no further work until this matter is all cleared up. Second, you are to follow the county building code to the letter of the law. Start the process by applying for a permit. Don't do anything more here until you've complied with everything required for the permit, including clearance from the Michigan Department of Environmental Quality. You've been down this road before. If you don't cooperate, you will be subject to both civil penalties and criminal charges. I'm sure you know that a felony conviction will put you out of office and prevent you from seeking one again for 20 years."

"Sheriff, you're wasting my time. The building is already down. I'm going to bury what's left at the sand quarry on my farm."

"You are going to follow the law like anyone else. The county or the DEQ will tell you how to dispose of these materials."

Ray took out his iPhone and started taking pictures. After a few moments he looked over at Feilen. "You are not to touch anything here until all the requirements of the county building code and state law have been fulfilled. It would give me no pleasure to have to arrest a member of the county commission, but if you deviate from statute law in any way, you will be arrested and charged."

Ray took a few more pictures, and then he and Glenn slowly walked back toward the county road.

"Think he'll comply?" she asked as soon as they were out of earshot.

"Hell no. Like he said, he's going to try to get rid of the contents of that truck. I imagine you saw the asbestos siding that was part of the gable ends?"

"Yes."

"The tags on the truck are out of date, so we will have a reason to pull him over. Then we will go to the prosecutor and figure out how to deal with this character."

"When do you think this will go down?"

Ray looked at his watch. "I'd give them 15 minutes for coffee and cigarettes, then another hour or so. Like Melvin said, they are almost done. He'll be trying to get the trash up to his sand quarry and disposed of as quickly as possible. I'll have a car at each end of this road waiting. Let's get a cup of coffee. I'll need your expertise as soon as we make the stop."

"How do you know it's going to happen like this?"

"I've seen him in operation before. The law doesn't apply to him."

47

Ray sat at the gray metal table in the interview room. Al Tenny, seated across from him, was slouched in the black plastic chair. Ray checked to make sure the video equipment was running and then, holding a plastic laminated sheet, read through the boilerplate interrogation guidelines, inserting the time, place, date, and Tenny's and his names. Then he asked, "Were you informed of your Miranda rights at the time of your arrest?" Ray looked at the yellow tobacco stains on the fingers of Tenny's right hand. The small room was beginning to reek of tobacco, booze, and soiled clothing.

"Yeah, I guess so."

"Mr. Tenny, you were stopped at approximately 10:00 this morning. The vehicle you were driving did not have a valid license plate, and you could not produce a driver's license or proof of insurance. Is that correct?"

"Whatever."

"The arresting officer also noticed the smell of alcohol. You consented to a breathalyzer test and blew a 1.4."

"Is that all?"

"I inspected the truck after you were brought to jail. It was almost empty. I thought Melvin would've filled it before he sent you off to dump the contents."

"I do what I'm told. Melvin always says, 'You're not paid to think, you're paid to follow orders.'"

"So what were his orders?"

"Can I smoke?"

"No. The orders, Al?"

"I was to wait around till you were long gone. Then I was to sneak out the rear entrance and take the back roads to the quarry. He wanted me to burn the trash and bury it. Then Melvin said I should come back and park the truck where you saw it this morning. He said if we made it look like we weren't doing anything more, you'd get off our ass."

"There's more to this story then you're telling me."

"Sheriff, you nailed my sorry ass. I confess. Turn me over to the prosecutor. I'll take the jail time. I just want to be out by deer season."

"Where did the junk come from?"

"It was inside that old building Melvin just tore down. I dragged it out and put it in the bucket of the end loader. Melvin dumped that into the truck before he started smashing the place to pieces."

"Al, I had a good look at that stuff. A couple of old mattresses, some worn-out clothes and shoes, a few pots and pans, some broken dishes, beer cans. What's this that all about? Was someone living in there?"

"Maybe. Sometime. I don't know. Let's get this over, Sheriff. I don't know anything. My job is to run the gravel pit. Melvin told me not to say nothing about the other stuff."

"But there was someone living in that building earlier this year. Am I right?"

"I wouldn't know."

"Jeans, shirts, lots of beer cans, empty cigarette packs. Looks like the things a couple of men might have. We even found a bible, Spanish edition."

"I don't know. He doesn't tell me much. I run the gravel pit. And I shut up about the rest of it."

"Al, it looks like Melvin was into some deep stuff. There were a couple of men living in that building sometime this summer, weren't there?"

"I wouldn't know."

"And Melvin had you load up the things they left behind and, like you told me, you were supposed to burn them and bury them."

"It was just junk. People come, people go. Melvin hires laborers from time to time. Lots of people have lived there over the years."

"Migrants?"

"Yeah, sometimes."

"Are they legal?"

"Not my job to check passports."

"When does rifle season open?"

"Six weeks, something like that. But I hunt bow season, too."

Ray looked down at his notes, slowly glancing over the contents of several pages. Then he raised his gaze. "Al, the DUI and other charges are small time. You understand that?"

"Yeah."

"I need to separate that from what I'm talking to you about now, the things in the dump truck, the belongings of two men. What we're looking at here is destruction of evidence and obstruction of justice. These will be federal charges. Later today or tomorrow you will questioned by some FBI agents. We're not talking about a few months in the county, you're looking at some serious time in a federal prison, perhaps most of the rest of your life."

Ray let his comments hang for a while, then said, "Tell me about the men who lived there."

"Okay, okay…nothing to tell really. Couple of little guys, Mex I think. They were only around for a few months."

"Did you talk to them? Did they have names?"

"They couldn't speak English. Melvin, he had their names. I think one was called Flaco, or something like that. The other was called Gordy or Gordo. Melvin had me bring them food sometimes when he was away. You know, beans, rice, ground beef, tortillas, crap like that. And beer. Lots of beer."

"Did you take them to town or anywhere else."

"No, Melvin, he wanted them to stay hidden. I just thought they were illegals. You know, trying to hide from the INS."

"What were they doing?"

"They were building stuff."

"What kind of stuff?"

"I don't know. I picked up lumber for them from time to time. Pine, thin pine boards. Melvin, he was ordering it from a couple of little sawmills in Karlin and south of T-ville."

"What were they building?"

"Boxes, crates, I don't know. Melvin said it was tourist junk. I saw the guys carrying some of the boxes over by the old cannery buildings. But then Melvin made it clear he didn't want me snooping around."

"When did you last see these two men?"

"End of the summer. Late August, maybe."

"Did you ask Melvin where they went?"

"No. Like I said, people come, people go. And he's real touchy. I learned not to ask questions."

"The old cannery buildings on the property, tell me about them."

"The big one, that was a storehouse for the canning plant back in the day. It's got the loading docks and all. Melvin used to rent it to a moving company for storage."

"Anything in it?"

"Just a bunch of junk, last I saw. I haven't been in there for years. Melvin, he keeps everything locked up like there's something worth stealing."

"How about the building next to it?"

"That was the canning plant. That's been closed for about as long as I can remember. There was a bottling line in there, too, once upon a time."

"For what?"

"Don't you remember the signs? 'Feilen's Famous Cherry Drink, a Northern Michigan Favorite.'"

"I think I missed it."

"Lucky you. I think they made it from the leftovers of the canning operation. Cherry juice and sugar. Sold it to tourists. Health department closed them down after a bunch of people got the runs one summer. There used to be a freezer plant, too. That burned down when I was a kid. They were pretty much out of the business by then."

Ray looked back at the material in the folder. "I see you were once charged with arson."

"Got reduced to a misdemeanor, Sheriff, you know that. Hell, it was just an old hunting cabin not really worth anything. Didn't mean to burn it down. And I wasn't alone. I was just too drunk to run away when the cavalry came rolling in."

"Where were you last week, Al?"

"In the U.P."

"Doing what?"

"I have a cabin north of the bridge."

"When were you there?"

"Went up Monday, came back Friday or Saturday sometime."

"Anyone see you?"

"Waitress at the Island Bar in Hessel. I was there every night."

"Did you pay with cash or use a credit card?"

"Cash, but I used an ATM. They got one in the bar."

"What were you driving?"

"An old Dodge Durango. It belongs to the business."

"You wouldn't know anything about a small dog, would you?"

"What are you talking about?"

"Someone was seen dropping off a dog in St. Ignace."

"What's the charge? Animal cruelty?"

"Tell me about it."

"I stopped by to get a check before heading north. Melvin had this stray up at the office. He told me to get rid of it. Made some joke about target practice. He sorta bullied me. Wouldn't give me the check till I promised to kill the dog. Nice dog. Rode in my lap all the way north. Thought about keeping it, but I knew it would find a home. Dropped it off in St. Ignace when I stopped for cigarettes."

"We need to find your boss. Where should we start?"

"I just look after the gravel pit. He doesn't tell me nothing."

"Don't play dumb, Al. You've been hanging with him for decades."

"Look, he's a restless SOB. Sometimes he drives to town three or four times a day. He just can't stay put."

"Women friends?"

"They come and go. He's got a mean streak, that's why they don't last long. He can only play nice so long, and then he gets pissed and slaps them around. But like I keep telling you, he doesn't tell me anything. Back in the day we were friends, but now that he's a big shot on the county board, I'm just a gofer."

"What's he driving these days?"

"Beemer of some kind. Black, and that new Dodge pickup, too. A monster truck."

"How about boats?"

"Mel's got all the toys."

"Boats, Al, boats?"

"He's got a bass boat with a big assed Merc and a Zodiac, Merc on that, too."

"Guns?"

"All the toys, Sheriff, all the toys."

"Handguns, rifles…?"

"Assault, too. Likes to fire them at the gravel pit. Thinks he's a frigging Rambo."

"How about martial arts."

"That, too. Picked it up in the military. Back in the day he used me as his sparring partner."

"The money, where's all the money coming from, Al? He always looked like he was just getting by."

"Last couple of years he's been into something new. Beats me what it is."

"Drugs?"

"I don't know."

"Where's his office?" Ray asked.

"It's up in the old farmhouse. Not an office like a real one, just a space off the kitchen, a computer and file cabinets."

"And he lives there, also?"

"Off and on. He has a condo in town. Bought it for a girlfriend. When that went sour, he took the place over. I think he sorta divides his time."

Ray looked up at the camera. "This concludes the interview."

"What's going to happen to me now, Sheriff?"

"To begin with, a stay in the county jail until we get this all sorted."

"If you lock his sorry ass up, don't put him near me. I'm scared of the bastard."

48

Ray found a copy of a news photo on his desk with a yellow post-it on the top.

Thought you'd find this interesting. S.

He looked carefully at the image. An eighteen-wheeler lay on its side in a ditch. A shipping container lay with one of its doors open, exposing the badly damaged contents. Ray pulled a magnifying glass from a drawer and focused on the interior of the container. He could see wooden boxes. Most were smashed, exposing what appeared to be wine bottles. His gaze moved down to the caption.

Icy roads claim another. Owners cry over spilt wine. Contents a total loss.

With the help of the glass, he studied the men standing near the back of the truck. He could clearly make out Geoffrey Fairfield.

At the bottom of the page, Sue had penciled in the complete citation. *Benzie County Observer*, February 23.

Ray looked again at the splintered boxes and shattered bottles in the container. He leaned back in his chair, closed his eyes for a few seconds, and visualized the pieces of the puzzle slowly coming together. Then he was on his feet, loosening the knobs at the ends of the whiteboard, and rotating it 180 degrees to a clean surface.

He listed all the things that needed to be accomplished. Placing the items in rank order, then revising the list as he rethought their importance.

- APB Feilen
- Contact FBI
- Search Warrants, all Feilen property
- Surveillance

"What's going on?" asked Sue.

"Perfect timing," he answered as he continued to add items to the list. "We'll divide these out. There's a lot that needs to be quickly accomplished."

A few hours later they were standing in the musty interior of the main storage building of Feilen's Fruit Processing. A line of shipping containers filled part of the building adjacent to the shipping dock.

Ray struggled with the locking handle on the door of the nearest container, finally pulling one door open, then unlatching and opening the other door. Then he pulled away sheets of foam packaging material, exposing rows of wooden boxes. With Brett Carty's help, he pulled one from the top center, set it on the floor, and then scouted around for a screwdriver.

"What am I looking for?" asked Sue, her hands on an iPhone.

"A bottle of Bordeaux, the product of one of France's most famous chateaus," said Ray, holding out the bottle. "Make sure you get the year right, 2008. "

They stood for a few moments in silence as she keyed in the information.

"I don't believe this," she said, holding the screen in their direction.

"$2,700 for a bottle of wine. So I'm looking at thirty-two grand in that one box. What's this all about?" asked Carty. "Is this stuff real?"

"Let's get into the next building. I think we'll have an answer very quickly," said Ray as he led the way toward the connecting hallway. The canning area was littered with debris. The old canning and bottling equipment had been pushed and piled against one wall. A complex stainless steel machine stood in the center of the room. Clean, empty bottles filled a conveyer on one side of the apparatus.

Cardboard boxes filled with new wine bottles stood in stacks near that end of the machine. At the other end were wire racks with a small number of bottles, and beyond that a few damaged wine cases.

"It's all here," said Ray. "A state of the art bottling machine, a variety of glass bottles, labels, corks, foils, cases."

"You wouldn't have to be a rocket scientist to pull this off," observed Carty.

"No," Ray made a sweeping gesture with his hand, "most of what you need is probably easily available on the web. Recreating the labels would probably be a challenge. You might need a high-end scanner and printer, but even that would only be a few thousand."

"Labels, lots of different labels," said Sue, looking over a nearby workbench.

"The right bottle, label, cork, and foil. Just add some good wine, and you might be able to fool the uninitiated."

"Who would that be?" asked Sue. "Maybe someone like me, but not people who've got the bucks to buy this kind of stuff."

"Export. Emerging markets where new billionaires want the world's most exclusive luxury products. I read an article in the *Times* last winter about the shortage of premium wines. Looks like Feilen and friends have figured out how to help with the problem."

"Come on, Ray," said Sue, "that creep is a loser. He couldn't have pulled this off without a lot of expert help and some serious money."

"True. Now we need a link to the money and brains." He motioned toward a line of large plastic tanks. "Those bulk containers, where do you think they came from?"

"Ursidae?"

"My guess, too. I wish they had that written on the side. I think they are common across the industry." He paused for a moment. "We should carefully back out of here so we don't further contaminate the scene."

"Agreed."

"How long could they have gotten away with this," asked Brett Carty once they were outside the warehouse, standing in the warm autumn sunshine.

"Not too long. Maybe they were in the process of winding this one down. But in there you saw the key element, the motive: counterfeit wine, counterfeit wine worth millions. I wonder how many loaded shipping containers have come out of here. Now we have to capture Feilen and make sure Lovell doesn't do a runner," said Ray.

"Do you think this stops with Lovell? I mean, Ursidae is owned by an international beverage consortium. Wouldn't they be perfectly positioned to facilitate this kind of scam?" asked Sue.

"Yes, but would it be worth the risk?" said Ray.

49

Ray pulled on a bulletproof vest and helmet, then reached back into the trunk for a military-style Colt carbine. Turning to Brett Carty, he said, "Remain here until backup arrives. Then cover the rear of the building. The shooter might try to escape out the back."

Using the cars in the crowded parking lot of the Ursidae Winery for cover, Ray and Sue quickly moved toward the main entrance of the building, the sound of gunfire echoing from the interior. The pavement and lawn near the building were filled with terrorized people, many bleeding, most struggling to get to cars and waiting buses.

They stood for several seconds on opposite sides of the main doors of the tasting room. As some of the last stragglers fought their way out of the building, they slipped in, finding cover behind counters and a bar area. The automatic gunfire continued in a distant part of the building.

Ray looked around as he carefully started moving through the room, occasionally glancing back at Sue. Much of the interior had been demolished by the hail of sprayed bullets. Shards of glass from shattered wine bottles and stemware covered the counters and floor. Wine dripped from the remains of display cases. Ruby spouts poured from the neat stacks of oak barrels that lined one wall. The air was thick with the smell of wine and the fetor of burnt gunpowder.

Ray moved to the double doors at the far end of the tasting room that opened to the bottling area. He pushed one of the doors partially open, quickly scanned the next room, and dove forward finding cover behind a pallet of wine cases. Looking back toward the door, he motioned Sue in during a respite of gunfire. The floor of the basketball court-size room was covered with wooden pallets, each stacked with cardboard boxes. Wine poured from bullet-torn boxes, some sagging, others collapsing. He spotted Feilen at the far end of the room tossing away an empty magazine, pulling another from a backpack, and slamming it into his rifle. Feilen swung the muzzle toward Ray and casually sprayed the area in an arching motion, bullets tearing into the cardboard boxes and ricocheting off the cement walls.

Ray waited until the shooting stopped, then cautiously peered around the corner. He saw just the top of Feilen's head as he disappeared down a stairway.

Then Ray heard more gunfire, reverberating up from the floor below. He motioned to Sue, pointing toward an exit—steel double doors, one pushed completely open, the other barely ajar. He made a second gesture, pointing down toward the walkout level of the building. Then he trained his rifle on the area where he last saw Feilen, watching peripherally as Sue slid out of the building.

He moved forward toward the stairway. As he peered into the lower level, bullets came up in his direction, rebounding off the steel risers, punching holes in the clear Lexan™ sheets that formed the sides of the stairway from the handrails to the stringers. From a protected position, Ray swung a heavy, floor to ceiling security gate across the opening to the stairwell, secured it with a hasp, and then pushed open an exit door and cautiously slid down the steep berm on the side of the building. He paused for a moment, breathing deeply, his ears ringing from the constant pummeling of gunfire. Then he crept around the berm.

Sue stood on the berm across from him. Between them, at the back of the building was a wide loading dock. A lone FedEx van idled on the wide expanse of concrete that separated them. Ray moved farther along the sloping earth to get a better view of the rear of the building. One huge overhead door was open. The regular entrance door next to it was closed.

Ray dropped to the side of the loading dock and started moving along the wall toward the open door. Sue mirrored his actions, coming from the other side. They both froze in place as the fusillade started again, finally ending with windows on the access door exploding outward and then the door opened. A woman in a FedEx uniform with terror flashing across her face, was pushed forward by Feilen, who held her tightly with one hand, an assault gun in the other. Feilen tossed her to the side as he jumped into the back of the vehicle. A few seconds later, the truck lurched forward in a tight turn toward the exit road.

Ray aimed at the truck, but then held his fire, seeing Brett Carty running toward the truck firing. Carty dived out of the way as the truck roared past him and continued to accelerate on the service drive as it sped away from them.

Ray, Sue, and Brett sprinted around the exterior of the building toward their vehicles, Ray yelling instructions into his radio to the dispatcher. Carty reached his patrol car first and within seconds was weaving his way through the arriving emergency vehicles. Sue and Ray were soon on the road following his lead. Ray could see the FedEx vehicle ahead of them on the long, straight undulating highway as the two police vehicles gained on the slower truck.

"Central, blockade access to the school complex and the highway. Put the schools in lockdown."

"What's he going to do?" asked Sue.

"Don't know. The man has nothing to lose."

By the time they reached the long curve in the road near the south end of the village, they were less than 100 yards behind Feilen. A police car was parked at an oblique angle across the entrance to the school complex. Ray could see an officer taking cover behind the vehicle.

Feilen appeared to be headed in the direction of the main highway, but at the last second he turned toward the high school, smashing into the left fender of the police car, and violently pushing it out of his way.

They followed the battered truck past the long line of buses parked at the front of the school waiting for the end of the school day, Feilen accelerating again as he rounded the side of the building, turning again as he hit the large paved area at the rear of the building next to the industrial arts area.

Ray could see that the van was heading full speed for the auto shop's tall garage door. There wasn't a hint of braking as the truck crashed into and through the door, stopping suddenly, violently. The rear wheels appearing to briefly lift off the ground.

On foot, they raced toward the wreckage, reaching the rear of the vehicle just as it was engulfed in flames.

Ray dashed to a nearby access door and smashed through the wired safety glass window with the butt of his rifle. He reached through the window and opened the door. After pulling a fire alarm, he moved to the entrance of the tool crib, pounding on the thick steel door. "Fire, fire, get out now!"

The door opened a crack, and then was pulled wide when the teacher recognized Ray. Two dozen frightened teenage boys, followed by their teacher, scampered out of the exit.

Ray glanced at the wreckage. The front of the FedEx truck had collapsed on impact as it rammed the school district's dump truck standing just inside the closed garage door. Flaming liquids were spreading across the shop floor. Seconds after he escaped the building, the whole interior exploded in flames.

They moved away from the building, teachers and other adults in front of them shepherding students to the far edges of the school grounds, away from the fire and the arriving emergency vehicles.

Breathless, Ray stood and watched.

"What was he thinking?" asked Sue.

"I don't know, maybe a hostage...." His voice trailed off.

"If this had happened a few minutes later, just after dismissal time."

"I don't want to think about it. We were all lucky."

50

Ray, standing at the side of Marty Donaldson's hospital bed, looked across at Mary Donaldson, who was seated on the other side holding his hand. "Is he behaving?" Ray asked.

"He has no choice. Plus he seems to go out of his way to please some of those pretty young nurses. It's when he gets home, that's what's worrying me. The doctors have made it clear that he's got to take it easy. He doesn't know how to do that. It's going to be hard on both of us."

"So, Sheriff," asked Marty, "you got this all sorted out?"

"We're still tying up loose ends, but I think we have a fairly clear idea of who the major players were and what motivated them."

"And it all started with the woman I found, Gillian Mouton?"

"The whole scheme, the production of counterfeit wine, was a house of cards waiting to collapse. But Gillian provided the catalyst to bring everything to a head."

"I don't understand."

Ray stood silently for a long moment thinking about where to start. "The production of counterfeit wine had been going on for several years, a trickle at first and then a steady flow. We found all the information in Feilin's office: letters of credit, shipping invoices, hard copies of emails. The FBI has taken custody of all material. Seems, among other things, Lovell and Feilen never bothered to pay the federal tax on alcohol."

"Imagine that." said Donaldson.

"Lovell started small, shipping a container of fraudulent wine every three months. When he saw how successfully his scam was working, he started to get greedy, moving from four containers a year to about a dozen. A trade group representing a consortium of major French chateaus had become increasingly aware of the flow of counterfeit copies of their products being marketed in China. I don't know the basis of this, but they were sure the counterfeit wine was coming from the United States. Gillian, among others, was enlisted in the hunt for the source of the counterfeit wine, with the promise of a huge reward.

"In the months before her death, Gillian was crisscrossing the country, visiting wineries similar to Ursidae, places that would have the capacity and know-how to produce high quality imitations. And once she was up here and had a good look around, it was clear that Ursidae was the only winery in this region that had the capacity to pull this off. But once she had a look around, she couldn't figure out how he was pulling it off. There was too much security and too much corporate oversight. I think her investigation was almost stalled at the time she was killed. She never anticipated Lovell having access to another winery, the long deserted processing plant owned by Melvin Feilen.

"Anyway, Phillip Lovell immediately understood the threat that Gillian posed to his multi-million dollar moonlighting gig. He also knew the house of cards was starting to fall, and he needed an exit strategy. He only had a few containers left. As soon as they were gone, he would be off to distant climes. First he had to get rid of Gillian, then he needed to keep the police occupied for just a few more weeks."

"Why my vineyard?" asked Donaldson.

"Feilen was following Gillian. She happened to stop there, thinking your son Randy was going to meet her. As it turned out, Randy didn't turn up, providing Feilen with a perfect location for the crime. So first there was Gillian, and then her stepbrother. Lovell was afraid that Gillian might have shared her suspicions with Gregory Mouton."

"But what about the other two who were killed?"

"Geoffrey Fairfield was an independent insurance adjuster. In February he investigated an accident where a truck slipped off the highway down in Benzie County. The container was filled with wooden cases branded with the name of a famous French burgundy. Fairfield figured out what was going on. You've heard the old line about 'everyone has a price.' It looks like they bought Fairfield's silence. But at the end his knowledge was too dangerous, and he had to be taken out. Sherry Mouton was probably collateral damage, just at the wrong place at the wrong time."

"And those two bodies found on North Manitou?"

"They were carpenters, brought in to construct the wine boxes and help with the bottling. We found everything in Feilen's buildings: woodworking tools, branding dies to mark the fake crates, corks, bottles, foils, and labels. I can't see that those men posed any real threat to this scam. As far as we know they didn't speak any English and would have probably disappeared south of the border after they were paid for their work. But I think Feilen had become addicted to large amounts of easy money. He must have seen them as a possible threat that could be easily eliminated. In fact, they were the first two victims. After that, my theory is that Feilen saw killing as the best way to eliminate threats.

"Phillip Lovell, on the other hand, has proved to be unusually talkative. We got lucky finding him. Canadian customs picked him up in Sarnia. They found him in the trunk of his girlfriend's convertible. You would have thought an experienced world traveler would have come up with a better plan.

"While he admits to setting up the business, he claims that other than that, he's a complete innocent. Early in the game he had contracted with Feilen to rent his buildings, and Feilen, once he figured out what was going on, blackmailed his way into taking over much of the operation. Lovell says he knows nothing about any of the homicides, but he says he had a sense Feilen was a psychopath. He was afraid of him."

"What's going to happen with the winery, Ursidae?"

"The place is swarming with suits from their corporate offices doing damage control. They've brought in a team of forensic accountants to try to uncover how Lovell was able to pull this off without anyone discovering what was going on. The top management is doing its best to distance themselves from the fraud. They've been guarded, but quite helpful with the investigation. They want to make sure they end up totally clean, untainted by this whole racket.

"The winery is temporarily closed, and one of the managers told me they may be putting the facility on the market. She said it's never produced the expected profits, and selling it off would provide a clean break from the scandal."

"We were victims, too," said Mary. "The worry and upset almost killed Marty. We were afraid the boys might have gotten involved in something."

"What happens now?" asked Marty.

"We complete our investigation and assemble all of the information for the prosecutor. That's a pretty massive job. We're also cooperating with federal prosecutors who will handle the murders of the two carpenters."

"Any idea as to their identities?"

"Sadly, no. We've reached out to the migrant community through Father Sanchez. No one seems to have any information. Our suspicion is they are illegals Feilen found through a labor contractor using the Internet. I've learned that you can order the kind of labor you need, and they are delivered to your facility. Someone somewhere is waiting for their husband or brother or father or son to return from up north with a bit of hard-earned cash to help the family. Their deaths are just one more tragic piece in this horrendous chain of events."

A long silence followed. Finally Marty said, "I'm almost embarrassed to ask, but the wine, is it any good?"

"All I can tell you is that Lovell said he fooled most of the experts."

"And the grapes, were they local?"

"Again, according to Lovell, some of the juice was local, much of it came from California. He bragged about his skill at blending."

51

They were on the water early, Hanna and Ray. The big lake was still a gently sloping plain that stretched to the horizon. Soft mauve from the sunrise streaked the surface of the water.

They headed toward the Manitous, small bow wakes peeling away as the kayaks sliced through the water. The sun crept up during the two-hour crossing, the features of the once distant shore coming into focus.

There was little conversation along the way, just the rhythm of paddles as they moved at a leisurely pace. Hanna, leading the way, landed on a narrow patch of sandy beach below the old lighthouse, pulling her boat onto the shore, then wading into the water and catching Ray's bow.

Seated on a concrete wall at the front of the lighthouse, Hanna poured coffee from a thermos and then carefully extracted two croissants from a watertight plastic container.

"Dark chocolate, or dark chocolate with marzipan?"

"Why don't you cut them in half?" Ray asked.

"Too easy."

Ray sipped his coffee and peered toward the mainland, indistinct in the early morning haze. He thought about the carnage of the last several weeks.

Hanna pulled the knife from her PFD and divided the pastries. She handed Ray his portion using the top of the container as a dish. "You okay?"

"Yes," he answered. "I'm just in recovery mode."

"It's interesting watching you during one of these investigations. Not that you're ever excessively effusive, but you become so quiet. You seem very focused, very little else gets through." Hanna paused, her tone lightened. "Except eating, of course. Put some great food in front of you, and you're suddenly with the living."

"I'm always trying to figure it out, trying to visualize the person's world, trying to find a motive," he answered, still gazing at a far horizon. "And then, like this last case, I'm always wondering how I might have done things differently. Could I have solved this faster and prevented some of these deaths?"

"So much for professional distance."

"I know you've struggled with similar things."

"True, even when the patient is unsalvageable. It was especially bad in Iraq. They were all so young, most just at the beginning of adulthood. As you know, I came back shattered. But even here, working with people who have lived long, full lives. So many aren't ready to go and…I do what I can. But in your case, you did figure it out and bring things to an end."

"But not before seven people died. And my nightmare scenario almost happened, a psychopath with an assault rifle in a school."

"So what was going on with this guy…?"

"Feilen? Probably need to talk to one of your colleagues in psychiatry. I remember him from high school. He was four years my senior, the mean kid in black leather with the beater hotrod. He wasn't on my radar again until he got on the county board. I don't know how he and Lovell got involved, but it appears that Feilen was willing to do the dirty work to protect a gold mine, including killing anyone who posed a threat to their enterprise. We're still just looking at the tip of the iceberg, but this counterfeiting operation produced millions of dollars, riches that Feilen couldn't even imagine. But leaving a trail of dead bodies is not a good long-term plan. Feilen was too dumb to see that."

"How long could they have continued if…"

"The end was near. Lovell had an exit plan in place. His millions are probably safely offshore somewhere. Maybe he even had a plan to make Feilen take the fall."

"All for a bag of gold." Hanna pushed her legs out in front of her and looked out at the water. "Do you ever think about future generations…children, grandchildren?"

"I think about the kids now and the world they will be inheriting. Look at this scene in front of us. Will they have this to enjoy in a hundred years? If I had a magic wand to fix all the things that are wrong…, but I don't. So I do what I can to keep the social contract in place in this tiny corner of the universe."

"Recently I've been thinking about children." She went silent for a long moment. "The alarm in my biological clock seems to have gone off. Then I think about the world they might inherit, and that gives me pause."

Ray pushed up on an elbow and looked at Hanna. "I can give you some grim lines from Matthew Arnold."

"Go ahead."

Ah, love, let us be true
To one another! for the world, which seems
To lie before us like a land of dreams,
So various, so beautiful, so new,
Hath really neither joy, nor love, nor light,
Nor certitude, nor peace, nor help for pain;
And we are here as on a darkling plain
Swept with confused alarms of struggle and flight,
Where ignorant armies clash by night.

"He must have been a joy to spend time with," Hanna responded. "You're a lot better company. He probably couldn't cook either."

"Arnold was lamenting the loss of religious certitude. What I take from the lines is the importance of holding onto and being true to the people we love. Humankind has always been on the edge of disaster, much of it of our own creating. Somehow we escaped a nuclear holocaust, but the climate...." Ray looked over at Hanna. "When are you going to Palo Alto?"

"What was the line? About love, the one you quoted."

"Ah, love, let us be true to one another!"

"I like that," said Hanna. "We can't control much, but we can choose to be true to one another." She pulled Ray close, held him tightly.

Author's Note—It Takes a Village

Larry Mawby, the always affable dean of northwest Michigan wine producers and the maker of award winning sparkling wines. Larry walked me through the process from vineyard and crusher to bottling and corking. (http://lmawby.com)

Madeleine Vedel: a gifted fromagère and food and travel writer. Madeleine guided me through the process of making prize-winning goat cheese from udder to table. (http://www.cuisineprovencale.com)

Mike Green, a master of repair and restoration of classic wooden boats. Mike showed me the structure and mechanical layout of period Chris Craft runabouts. (http://www.maritimeclassics.com)

Tove Danovich, a gifted young writer, helped me find a perfect NY locale.

Heather Shaw, who has been part of this effort almost from the beginning. I am indebted to Heather for her extraordinary skills in every aspect of bringing a manuscript to print and her constant friendship and support over many years. (http://heatherleeshaw.businesscatalyst.com)

Kudos to Aimé Merizon, Barb Osbon, and Paula Stewart for proofreading and/or editorial suggestions.

My thanks to the many independent bookstores who have been handselling my titles for more than a decade.

Books in the Ray Elkins Series:

Summer People
Color Tour
Deer Season
Shelf Ice
Medieval Murders
Cruelest Month
Death in a Summer Colony
Murder in the Merlot